HUMAN FOR HIRE (3) — DEVIL'S GATE —

COLLATERAL DAMAGE INCLUDED

T.R. HARRIS

**Copyright 2022
by Tom Harris Creations, LLC**

**Edited by
Lionel Dyck
Sherry Dixon**
Grammarly
And of course…
Nikko, the Grammar Dog

This is a work of fiction. Names, characters, places, brands, media and incidents are either the product of the author's imagination or are used fictitiously. All rights reserved, without limiting the rights under copyright reserved above, no part of this publication may be reproduced, stored in or introduced into a retrieval system, or transmitted, in any form, or by any means (electronic, mechanically, photocopying, recording, or otherwise) without the prior written permission of both the copyright owner and the above publisher of this book.

HUMAN FOR HIRE

— DEVIL'S GATE —

IN A ROUGH AND TUMBLE GALAXY,

ruled by gun and muscle...

When you need the very best mercenary, bounty hunter, bodyguard or just straight muscle, you find a ...

HUMAN for HIRE

1

Callie Morrison came out from taking a Navy shower aboard her cramped, tiny starship, the *Angel*, feeling refreshed physically, even as her mind was clouded emotionally. In the cockpit, she stretched in all her naked glory, knowing there was no one to see through the viewport for light-years in every direction. It had been a while since she luxuriated in such a way, hoping the brief, enveloping cocoon of warm, soothing water would calm her troubled mind. Unfortunately, it didn't. Instead, it made her feel even more guilty.

As she began toweling off, she struggled with her conflicted emotions. This wasn't like her. She was usually a tough-as-nails, take-no-prisoners kind of gal, justified by years as a successful con-artist in a *them-against-her* contest of wills and skills. And she always came out the winner. That wasn't hard to understand, seeing that she was a Human and all her marks were aliens. It was hardly a fair contest. But this time it was different.

This time she'd screwed over a fellow Human.

And it was someone she really liked.

Callie snuggled into a thick cotton robe and tied the cord around her narrow waist. The material was comforting but it still didn't relieve her shame.

"Dammit!' she said aloud. "I deserve the credits!"

After all, it had been her operation from the beginning, an elaborate plan to rob one of the Big Five Banks in the galaxy. She not only researched the facility and its security systems, but she also constructed a detailed cover story that would leave her anonymous and free at the end. And then she went undercover at the bank for four long, grueling months. She hadn't held down a real job since she left Earth nine years earlier, so the time spent on the planet Tactori was excruciating. More than anyone else in the operation, she put in more time, effort and brainpower. Everyone else who came in afterwards were just bit players.

But Adam Cain was different. She really liked him and it crushed her usually hardened soul to see him so depressed and despondent after they left Bandors Bank on Tactori.

Oh, well, she shrugged. He'll survive; in fact, he'd

proved capable of that more than any other living being in the galaxy. And now he was headed back to Tel'oran. Sure, he and the company he worked for didn't make any money from their latest job; hell, Adam even ended up owing the bank a hundred thousand credits when all was said and done. But there would be other jobs, both for Adam and for Callie. It would just take a little time for her to work through her guilt.

She sat in the pilot's seat and stared out the viewport at a brilliant cluster of stars and nebulae off to her port side. She sighed, thinking what a beautiful sight it was … and how absolutely immune she was to it. Had nine years in space jaded her that much that she no longer felt the awe and wonder of journeying through the galaxy in a compact starship of her own? Was it that easy for even the glory of outer space to become … ordinary?

"Knock it off, Callie!" she yelled at herself, needing the sound of her voice to remind her what it was like to interact with another Human, if it was only her voice she was hearing.

She considered that for a moment. For the past three years, she hadn't even seen another Human until Adam appeared on the scene. Was part of her attraction to him simply from the fact that she was lonely and homesick? Nah! Adam Cain was a certifiable hunk of the first degree. An amazingly fit ex-Navy SEAL, who had been cloned back to his twenty-two-year-old-self, yet with all the experiences and confidence of a man approaching sixty who had done and seen everything. He was a truly unique person, and Callie had experienced him firsthand.

And yes, she screwed him over, and in more than the way she regretted.

It had only been two days since they went their separate ways, he back to Tel'oran and Starfire Security, and Callie heading for her semi-permanent digs on the planet Gavon near the Kidis Frontier. She attributed her melancholy mood to the freshness of the breakup after only a brief week-long affair. Give her another week, and she'd be completely over Adam Cain. At least she hoped so.

It was almost a relief when the proximity alarm sounded aboard the *Angel*, giving Callie something new to think about other than Adam Cain. She frowned at the contact on the nav screen. She was in open space, light-years away from the nearest settled star system. The odds of coming this close to another vessel were, well, astronomical.

Callie tapped the control stick, changing course by about five degrees. Sure enough, the following contact changed course with her.

She grimaced. She wasn't worried, just frustrated. Her ship was small, but it was almost all engines. She had dual Gravtec generators that were massively over-rated for the size of her ship, along with four focusing rings. She'd made the improvements a few years back after a particularly lucrative score and they'd paid dividends ever since. She was sure the *Angel* was the fastest ship in this part of the galaxy, if not the whole Milky Way.

But why was a ship following her? She trusted that Bandors Bank had lifted all warrants against her. Then she chuckled. Bandors wasn't the only party in the galaxy that she'd wronged. Not even close. So, this ship could be coming after her for any number of reasons. That was fine, let them try to catch up—

And that's when another alarm blared, signifying a second ship, this one coming in from port.

Okay, so a coordinated operation. That spoke of a more serious adversary. Still, it wouldn't make a difference. The *Angel* was cruising along at about half her top speed since it didn't pay to advertise one's true capacities. Best to play that close to the vest.

Callie let the ships approach, coming as close as they dared so as to not mix gravity-wells. And then she waited for the inevitable contact. It came only seconds after velocities were matched.

She opened the link.

"Identify yourselves and state your intentions," she demanded. "I am a private vessel breaking no laws."

A leathery, green-skinned creature came on the screen, alien yellow eyes staring unblinking at the Human.

"My identity is immaterial; our intention is to board your vessel and retrieve certain property."

"What property?"

"I believe you know of which I speak."

Callie pursed her lips. "I honestly don't have any idea what you're talking about." And she didn't. Not to any certainty.

"We are associates of the expired Mada Niac, part of his network of recovery agents and supporters."

Callie tensed. *Did they know?* And if so, how?

"I'm sorry about your associate, but I still don't know what you're talking about."

"We were in contact with Mada, knowing he carried within his vessel ten million energy credits. We also know that after taking your ship within his, certain events took place that resulted in your escape and the subsequent destruction of his vessel. Shortly thereafter, you and an associate returned eight million, four hundred thousand ECs to Bandors Bank."

"What does that have to do with anything? We negotiated with the bank for the return of credits in exchange for the lifting of all warrants. Mada spent some of the ten million before we recovered it, but the bank accepted the amount returned to them for payment in full. If you are acting on a writ surrounding that transaction, then please check your timestamp. You will find I have been cleared of any culpability."

"We do not represent Bandors. We represent ourselves."

"Then I don't know how I can help you."

"We know that Mada did not spend the credits you speak of. Therefore, we suspect that it was *you* who absconded with the shortage of one million, six hundred thousand ECs. That is the property we seek from you. Drop from light speed and allow us to recover these funds and you will be free to go."

"I don't have the credits. As I said, Mada spent them, not me. That's why there was a shortage."

"Impossible. We know for a fact that Mada had sophisticated weighing equipment aboard his vessel. He measured the credits accurately. He had ten million units. And yet, when you delivered the funds to Bandors, you were short. *You* took the credits. Do not deny it."

Well, shit, they had her pretty much dead to rights. That was exactly what happened. Feeling that she was owed at least a little of the money, she raided the security chest and stashed one-point-six million in the *Angel*, unbeknownst to Adam. She figured she deserved it more than him and his Juirean boss. In reality, it was her money, not theirs. So, she was really stealing from herself.

She smirked at the alien on the screen. "Okay, you got me. I admit it. I took the credits. But I'll be damned if I'm going to turn them over to you." Callie's hand moved toward the gravity-well controls, preparing to kick the *Angel* into high gear. Afterward, she may keep the alien on the screen just so she could see the startled look on his craggy face when she sprinted away—

A brilliant white flash filled the cockpit at almost the same time Callie's ship jerked to port. Alarms went off and lights flickered. Not waiting to do a diagnostic, Callie increased the dynamo effect through the generators. The *Angel* bolted away, but at only a fraction of the speed she was expecting.

A quick check of the systems revealed the awful truth. The *Angel* had been hit, not by a flash cannon bolt, but a high-intensity and targeted laser beam. Lasers were very effective short-distance weapons that, unlike flash cannon, traveled at the speed of light, magnitudes faster than the bolts. A beam had struck her starboard gravity generator, rendering it inoperable. This was catastrophic damage. It didn't mean that the *Angel* was now operating on half power, it was more like one third. The dual generators worked together to produce the dynamo effect, and without both operating, a single generator was ridiculously inefficient.

Callie checked her screens. As expected, the ship that had fired the laser was dead in space and would be for the next couple of hours as it recharged its batteries. That was the problem with laser weapons; they sucked up every spare watt onboard the ship. Unfortunately for Callie, there was another vessel to take up the pursuit.

And it wasn't much of an effort on their part. The second enemy ship pulled in behind her, placing its gravity-well tantalizingly close to the *Angel*. The g-well had an even more harmful effect on her forward progress, slowing the ship even more. Only Callie's well kept her from being sucked into the singularity located on her six. But even as the enemy's well served to tug on the *Angel*, Callie's helped pull the enemy ship along behind her, allowing it to expend less energy even as the *Angel* ate greedily into her reserves. The trailing ship was in no hurry to attack; they didn't have to. They would wait until her fuel pod was drained and then simply move into board the ship. And although the *Angel* had an adequate defensive system, the enemy didn't want to get into a shooting war. That might destroy the ship and the one-point-six million credits she had aboard.

What her enemy didn't realize about Callie, however, was that she was a planner. Over the years, she'd plotted out countless scenarios and what it would take to get out of even the hairiest of situations.

And that was why she had a plasma bomb aboard. Afterall, every red-blooded Human con-artist needed a plasma bomb aboard their vessel, right? It made sense. One never knew when it might come in handy.

Callie prepped the weapon for release. In her scenario, the bomb would only work if she were being followed closely by a starship in gravity drive. She would release the bomb, give it time to approach the event horizon of the following ship's microscopic singularity, and then she would detonate the bomb. The enemy well would dissolve and the rest would be history. Of course, she also had to dissolve her well almost simultaneously, else the bomb's blast field would be sucked forward instead of backward.

She checked the relative speeds. They were matched and the distances were correct. Of course, this tactic was merely theory; Callie had never actually tried it. *Oh well, better now than never.*

She released the bomb.

Five seconds later, she sent the detonation signal and dissolved her gravity-well.

The bomb exploded as planned, with the EM pulse overloading the enemy gravity-well and dissolving it in an instant. The trailing ship only had a split second to react before its forward momentum carried it into the blast zone. There was no time to raise shields, and the vessel's outer hull was stripped away by the intense heat. Pressurized compartments exploded outward from the escaping atmosphere, and only three seconds after the bomb exploded, a twisted and dead husk of a starship was all that still followed the *Angel* as the ship's momentum carried it along.

Callie checked the screens again. The first enemy ship was barely within range and still sitting motionless in space. But that wouldn't last much longer. Once their batteries were recharged, they would be coming after her with all the speed they could muster. And the *Angel* was still operating at only one-third capacity.

Callie couldn't remain out here. She had a sizeable lead but staying in space wasn't an option. She needed a safe harbor, someplace she could hide and affect repairs. She snickered. She had the money for the repairs. But she would need a way to fend off the pursuit that would undoubtedly follow her wherever she went.

There was only one option. In one way she welcomed it; in another, it was going to be awkward.

She was going to Tel'oran ... and back to Adam Cain.

2

Although Callie couldn't detect the enemy ship following her, she instinctively knew it was there. Tel'oran was the only logical planet for her to take her damaged starship. She figured she had about a six-hour head start. It wasn't a lot, but it would be enough for her to disappear into the metropolis of Dal Innis.

After landing at the main commercial spaceport for the city, she loaded the energy credits into a large backpack, and along with some personal items, she stepped outside the *Angel* and locked the ship. She kissed her hand and then laid it on the still warm hull, hoping she'd see the ship again. Undoubtedly, the aliens following her would gain entry and then tear the insides apart looking for the money. When that failed, they'd come looking for her.

Callie took a transport-for-hire across town to the executive spaceport where Adam said he kept the *Arieel*. It was more exclusive—at least for landing space; fortunately, the grounds were open to walk-in traffic without a security check. It took her fifteen minutes to find Adam's ship.

She huddled behind a nearby vessel, watching the *Arieel*. From the creaking and popping, it was evident that Adam had just arrived, having been in no hurry to get back to the planet to face his soon-to-be-irate boss. Callie wasn't anxious to walk up to the ship and knock on the door, especially not while she carried a backpack full of energy credits which, in an odd way, belonged to Adam. Internally, she still justified the theft, but her argument wouldn't hold water with Adam. Besides, she had no desire to let him know she had the money.

Adam came out of the side hatch and did a quick post-landing check of the starship. It was while he had his head stuck in a rear lifting jet nozzle that Callie made a mad dash for the *Arieel*. She bounded through the open airlock and headed aft. She knew the interior intimately and ducked into the secondary stateroom, the one Adam used mainly for storage. Slipping the backpack from her shoulders, she shoved the pack under the bunk. She relaxed. Now, she would wait for Adam to come back aboard and get settled in. Then she'd surprise him.

To enhance the surprise—and pleasure—of her return, Callie stripped down to her skimpy bra and panties. Hopefully, this would distract him from asking too many questions, at least until later. Besides, she would enjoy the diversion herself.

Adam came back in the ship and slipped into his stateroom where he remain for a full five minutes before a series of strong knocks came to the hull of the *Arieel*. Callie tensed and removed the MK-17 bolt launcher she had in the backpack. Had the enemy tracked her here already? Was she cornered, soon to shoot her way out of a mess?

Adam went to the airlock, and a moment later, Callie heard voices—Human voices—along with a raucous reunion of sorts. She pressed her ear against the metal door of the stateroom, able to clearly hear the conversation that took place in the common room down the hall. And the more she listened, the weaker her knees became.

Adam's guests were three old Human friends, and their visit was a surprise. From the tone of Adam's voice, he was suspicious of their arrival, as well he should. Having three Humans show up on one's doorstep—especially in this day and age—was unheard of. But it didn't take long for the reason for their visit to become known.

They were telling Adam about a bank that was rumored to be holding half a billion energy credits.

And this bank was in the Klin-controlled area known as the Devil's Gate. Of course, Callie knew of the Gate —everyone did—in fact, it was on the way back to the Kidis Frontier from here. She listened in awe as Adam's friends explained how the bank was behind enemy lines, and therefore, fair game for anyone who could rob it. As a confidence-woman of extraordinary skill, Callie couldn't agree more. She laughed softly as both she and Adam mouthed the same line in unison: *This could be the perfect crime.*

And then Adam said count me in. That was Callie's thought as well.

She reached for the door of the stateroom, but then hesitated. She was barely dressed and Adam didn't know she was there. And how would his friends react to know she'd be eavesdropping on their plans? No, she would have to be more subtle. It would be best if she were invited to join the caper than force herself into it. And that would involve manipulating Adam, alone, and without his buddies around.

She'd become distracted with her scheming, and when she returned to listening, something was happening.

3

Adam had only been on the planet for an hour and already he was getting ready to leave.

"General, get back to your ship. I'll be lifting as soon as I get another fuel pod. Give me a couple of hours."

"You really think this Tidus character will try to stop you from going after a half-a-billion in Klin energy credits? Those silver-skinned bastards just destroyed the Expansion and nearly exterminated the Juirean race. You would think he'd be all about some payback."

Adam grimaced. "That's not the point. He's concerned about the reputation of his company. He got pissed when I recently assassinated a planetary president and VP—"

"You did what?" General Todd Oakes asked incredulously.

"Hey, they had it coming. But that's not the issue here. Tidus doesn't want Starfire Security to be associated with assassins … or bank robbers. We're supposed to be an up-and-up company."

"I hope the double assassination paid well," Mike Hannon said wryly. He was the team's only 'official' alien assassin. Adam got the feeling he was more jealous than shocked.

"It would have, but I ended up killing my client as well. He deserved it, too."

"Holy shit," Oakes said. "No wonder *The Human* has such a reputation."

"You had to be there," Adam said impatiently. "But seriously, you guys have to go. Tidus knows I'm on the planet, and if I don't show up in his office within the next hour he's going to be all over me like stink on shit. I have preparations to make before we head for Devil's Gate."

Oakes nodded. "No problem. We'll head into orbit and wait for you there. Keep us informed."

The other three Humans left the ship, with Adam only a step behind. He had to score another fuel pod as soon as possible. The trip to Devil's Gate would take three weeks, and then he had no idea how long the operation would last or what resources he'd find there for fuel. They still had to go to General Oakes' confidential informant to get more information about the bank and the security measures. In fact, there was a whole slew of details that had to be worked out, and it didn't help that the responsibility for coming up with a viable plan had been dropped in his lap. And based on recent events, Adam's batting average wasn't that good. He was in a slump, and he knew it. After what happened on Osino and with the recovery fee, his confidence was shaken. But this was an operation strictly for Adam and his three Human friends. There was no client to satisfy before he could get paid. Of course, the risk was considerable, as was the potential payout. It was all a matter of risk-to-reward. And the potential payoff of half-a-billion energy credits dwarfed nearly all other concerns.

But first, Adam had to avoid Tidus.

Alone aboard the *Arieel*, Callie took the opportunity to find a secure place to hide her cache of energy credits. Although not officially a smuggler's hold, she located a panel in the cargo bay that could be removed, revealing a void between the bulkheads. The backpack fit nicely within. Afterwards, she went to the bridge to keep an eye out for Adam. Once he returned with the fuel pod, he would lift off immediately, wanting to avoid the Juirean Tidus at all costs.

She considered her timing, coming to the only logical conclusion. She would wait until they were in space before revealing her presence. And even then, she wouldn't disclose the fact that she knew of the bank job, unless it was absolutely necessary. She wanted him to ask her to join the team. It was the only way he—and the others—would accept her being aboard.

The fuel pod for the *Arieel* was a compact device only about three feet long by nine inches in diameter. It was a self-contained cold fusion reactor that would supply the power for the gravity generators, which in turn ran the focusing rings. The whole process seemed simple and straightforward, but Adam had been around long enough to know that the technology for such a device was light-years ahead of where Earth would be at this time if it hadn't been for the aliens coming to the planet. The ironic part: Those aliens had been the Klin, the same Klin who maneuvered the Juireans into attacking his homeworld—killing billions—and then later masterminded a series of galaxy-wide conflagrations that killed trillions, throwing the Milky Way back into the relative Dark Ages of galactic civilization.

That's why robbing the Klin of a shitload of energy credits would be so satisfying. If he survived the job.

Adam got back to the *Arieel* in only fifty minutes. He stored the fuel pod in the cargo bay; he didn't need it now, but he would soon. Then he checked his food stocks and then did a quick pre-launch walk-around. He was ready to go, and ahead of schedule.

Adam was surprised Tidus wasn't blowing up the commlinks asking where he was. It was customary after returning from a mission to report to headquarters. Besides, Adam supposedly had a million-and-a-half energy credits to turn over to the company as a recovery fee for the ten million he returned to Bandors Bank. And that was the reason Adam had to get out of town in a hurry. He didn't have the money. But that's another story.

With a sigh of relief, Adam slipped into the pilot's seat and called the tower, receiving permission to liftoff. He sighed visibly, knowing he was going to make it. He was going to get away before Tidus confronted him about the recovery fee, an event that would undoubtedly lead to him being fired from Starfire Security and the subsequent confiscation of company property, namely Adam's home, the starship he'd christened the *Arieel*.

With the departure coordinates locked in, Adam triggered the warm-up procedure for the lifting jets. They would only take five minutes to charge … if they had engaged. Instead, there was only silence.

Adam scrambled to check the system. All the lights were green—or *amber*, according to alien standards. He triggered the jets again, and again nothing happened.

"Dammit!" Adam yelled. "Not now!"

He unbuckled from the seat and ran for the engine room, at a loss as to why the engines weren't lighting. He was an adequate starship mechanic—something developed over years of experience piloting a variety of vessels across the universe—in fact, across *multi-*universes. But he was no expert by any shot. In the engine room, he checked every system he knew, finding everything to be in working order, right up to the point where the ship wouldn't start.

What the hell is wrong?

And then Adam abruptly slumped to the floor as reality struck him. It was the *only* answer. After all, the power system was fairly straightforward, it should be working. Unless someone placed a *kill switch* in the ship. And that someone had to be1 Tidus Fe Nolan, his Juirean boss.

There was already a hidden tracking device inside the *Arieel*, there to help find the vessel should it get stolen—as it had numerous times over the past three years. Stealing starships was as prevalent in the galaxy these days as horse thievery was in the Old West. The tracker was placed aboard at Adam's insistence. But a *kill switch*? That was new. Had Tidus placed it aboard the ship to prevent others from stealing it, or was it to prevent Adam from using the *Arieel* when Tidus didn't want him to? Adam already knew the answer. Tidus was shrewd and calculating: He did it to stop Adam from going rogue ... as the Human was about to do.

Adam returned to the bridge and called General Oakes to let him know what was going on.

"So, what are you going to do?" the gruff old military officer asked.

"I have something in mind, but it will probably mean a delay in going after the bank."

"How much of a delay?" the youngish Jay Williford asked in the background. Jay, General Oakes and Mike Hannon were aboard the general's starship and waiting for Adam in orbit

"Not too much, I hope. But this may turn out to be an advantage."

"How so?" Oakes asked.

"I'm not sure yet. I'll contact you after I've talked with Tidus."

Oakes shrugged. "We were counting on using your ship, Adam. Mine's a military vessel. It won't be allowed through the Gate."

"It's not over yet, General. Give me a few hours. I'll know more then."

"What choice do we have? Good luck."

Adam winked and grinned, a sign of outward

confidence that he didn't feel on the inside. Then, reluctantly, he left the *Arieel* and took his transport into Dal Innis to see Tidus. This was not going to be fun, not even close.

4

Tidus Fe Nolan was a seven-foot-tall, green-skinned alien with a four-foot-long grey ponytail running down his back. Twenty years ago, when he served as an Overlord in the Juirean Authority, his hair would have been more like a mane of bright blue that billowed out from his forehead and cascaded over his head and down his back. It added another foot to his stature and helped Juireans with their air of dominance. But after rebelling against the Authority and leaving in shame, he let the hair go back to its natural color, which was now silver-grey, and worn in the scraggily ponytail that was his current fashion statement.

But Adam wasn't focused on Tidus's grooming or wardrobe. Instead, he studied the alien's glowing yellow eyes for any clue as to how the meeting was to go. At the moment, the Juirean didn't seem upset, even with Adam's delay in showing up at the office. If not, then why did he activate the kill switch?

"So, buddy, how's it going?" Tidus asked. After years of operating as one of the top bounty hunters in the galaxy while working with Priority Acquisitions, Tidus was prolific with dozens of slang languages, including English, and even without the assistance of the translation bug everyone had embedded behind their ear. "Did you have a pleasant trip back from Tactori and Vosrum?"

Adam nodded slowly. "Yeah, it was fine." Something was up. This wasn't like Tidus.

"Good, glad to hear it." Then Tidus sighed and looked at his computer screen. It was turned away from Adam. "Boy, that operation with Bandors Bank was a real nailbiter, wasn't it? I'm glad you got your name cleared. It was touch and go there for a while. But now, I guess we have a little business to tend to."

"I don't have the recovery fee," Adam blurted. There was no easy way around it, so Adam chose to rip the Band-Aid off rather than pull it off a little at a time.

Surprisingly, Tidus didn't appear shocked—or mad.

"You don't have it? Is it back at your ship—eh, I mean *my* ship, since technically the *Arieel* belongs to the company?"

Adam shook his head. "Let me explain what happened."

Tidus leaned back in his chair and waved a hand at Adam. "Please do. I'm anxious to hear the story."

"Well, you know we got the credits back from Mada Niac and returned them to the bank. The agreement was a fifteen percent recovery fee."

"Hence, the one million, five hundred thousand credits I'm expecting."

"Well, it turns out Mada spent some of the money before we got it back, probably on a new batch of henchmen."

"How much was left?"

"About eight point four million."

Tidus leaned forward and typed on his computer. "That's okay. That still leaves one million, two hundred sixty thousand as a recovery fee."

Adam shifted nervously in his chair. "Unfortunately, that's not how the bankers saw it. They said they contracted for eight-point-five million and our recovery fee was anything above that."

Tidus frowned and looked at the numbers on the screen. "But that's more than the eight-point-four you returned to them. What are you trying to say, Adam?"

"I'm saying there is no recovery fee. And not only that, but they billed me for the other hundred thousand credits they were shorted. Dammit, Tidus, we didn't get anything, and I ended up owing money to the bank. This really sucks. I'm sorry."

Tidus stared at Adam, the expression on his face one of mild amusement.

Adam was confused and embarrassed, right up to the point he blurted out, "What the hell's wrong with you? Are you on drugs or something? I just told you the mission was a bust—in fact we went in the hole—and you just sit there with that cheeky grin. Get mad or something!"

"Why should I?" Tidus said calmly. "I've known about this from the beginning." And then the expression changed, and Tidus's face turned to stone. "That's right. Even before the bankers offered you terms on the payback of the hundred thousand ECs, they linked with me to ask about your credit rating."

"They … they *contacted* you?"

"That's right, and apparently they weren't happy with what I told them. That's why I ended up having to guarantee the loan. So, you see, Adam, we're both on the hook for the shortage."

"You bastard! Why didn't you tell me you knew?"

"Because I wanted to see if you'd be forthcoming with me. And you weren't. It's been almost two weeks since you left Tactori, and not a peep out of you about what happened. If you'd just been honest with me, I wouldn't be so mad."

"You don't seem mad now."

"That's because it's been weeks! Believe me, I have been mad, a lot madder than I am now. Now, I'm just disappointed."

Adam slumped in the chair. If he'd known Tidus was already aware of what happened, it would have relieved weeks of stress and anticipation. Again, Adam thought, *you bastard*.

"So, you've just been playing with me. And what about the kill switch on the *Arieel*? Just more games?"

"That was installed the last time you were here so your ship wouldn't get stolen so much. And you know, it would work better if you wouldn't wait to tell me about someone taking it until long after the fact. You have to stop keeping things from me, Adam. We're supposed to be friends. And more than that, I'm your damn boss!"

"So, you're not going to fire me?"

"How can I; you need to pay off your debts."

"I have a hundred thousand in savings—"

"Bullshit! You have thirty-eight thousand."

Adam was stunned. "You're tracking my bank accounts?"

"Don't be naïve, Adam. We're a security company. I need to know if my employees are in any financial trouble that might make them break the law, or even rob a bank or something."

Adam's stomach twisted into knots. Did he know

about Devil's Gate? Was the *Arieel* bugged? He didn't press the issue.

"Well, you know I'm good for it."

"You used to be, but your track record recently isn't that great."

"I'll make it up to you," Adam said quickly. "Let me check the Boards, find another job where we can each make some money."

"You aren't going to make a cent until the hundred thousand is paid, along with another nine hundred thousand."

"Nine hundred thousand? What's that for?"

"That's how much the company would have made from the one-point-five million credit recovery fee."

"Hey, that wasn't my fault! I had no way of stopping Mada from spending the credits."

Tidus shrugged. "That's true, but I don't really care. I feel after Osino—along with your other recent misadventures—you owe at least that much to the company. And if you don't like that, then you can consider it rent for the *Arieel*. That, or I will fire you and take back the ship. The choice is yours."

Defeated, Adam slumped deeper into the chair. "Yeah, whatever."

"So, we have a deal?"

Adam snorted and smirked.

"Good, now go find us a down and dirty bounty, something simple. I hate owing credits, especially to a cutthroat outfit like Bandors Bank. After that, we'll talk more about the nine hundred kay. That's how you Humans refer to it, as nine hundred kay?"

"Again, whatever."

Tidus grinned, something he'd learned to do after leaving the Juirean Authority. Normally, Juireans didn't smile. But this wasn't an expression of glee; it was more sadistic. "Now, hop to it, Mr. Cain. Go do your *Human* thing and make me some credits ... for a change."

5

After Adam left Tidus's office, he stopped and leaned against the wall. That didn't go exactly as planned, but in a way, it did. He still had a job and a place to live. And all he had to do now was find a nice little job located somewhere just outside the Devil's Gate. That would give him an excuse to be in the area. A quick score to get Tidus off his back, and then on to the Klin bank.

After that, Adam wouldn't give a damn how much he owed Tidus. Hell, he might even buy Starfire Security from the Juirean. Then Tidus would work for *him*. Now, that had a nice ring to it.

Adam appropriated an empty office and logged into the galactic database for bounties, bodyguard requests and other miscellaneous jobs available to people like Adam, freelance mercenaries and ex-military who would do just about anything for a credit. Known as the *Boards*, at any given time there were hundreds of thousands of job listings from across the galaxy.

Adam began by targeting a region. He always started this way, but usually to find assignments closer to home rather than farther away. The Devil's Gate was four thousand light-years from Tel'oran and would take three weeks to get there. Tidus would question why he picked a job so far away? Adam had to have an answer.

Since the Devil's Gate region was so far off the beaten path, there were literally thousands of listings still open. Nobody wanted to go out that far, even though most jobs paid an *inconvenience* bonus of a few thousand credits. There were the customary fugitive recovery posts—a heluva lot of them in fact—as countless criminals and renegades flocked to the area to avoid the rapidly re-organizing core of the galaxy that was less tolerant of their questionable activities.

And then there were hundreds of mercenary jobs. They paid well but took longer to come to fruition. Bodyguard jobs were plentiful and usually involved covering someone for a conference or a defined period of time. The problem, they didn't pay very well, not unless you were guarding a high-level politician or business being.

So, Adam was looking for something that wasn't only simple, but would also hold his interest. He knew he'd be distracted with planning the bank job, so he needed something that was not his normal forte.

His eyes fell upon a two-tiered listing, divided into a fee for information-only leading to an arrest, and then more if one was to bring the perpetrators to justice themselves. This was more of a law enforcement-type assignment and would involve the deputizing of the merc while on the planet. This piqued Adam's curiosity. It would be nice operating under official sanction for once.

It was an energy credit counterfeiting ring operating on the planet Lo'roan. Because of the technology involved in producing the universal credit chips, counterfeiting wasn't that common, but apparently, this ring was an exception. Adam read the details.

Subsequent investigations showed that the gang had the printing process down pat. But like most counterfeiting operations, the weak point was in the backing material. On Earth, it was the specialized paper used. For energy credits, it was the plastic masters. They were infused with hundreds of electronic countermeasures to assure authenticity and discourage counterfeiters. Add to this the fact that most establishments had sophisticated readers that could detect fake chips, and there wasn't much success in this type of crime. Even so, this gang was flooding the local market with fake chips that were almost as good as the real thing. According to the data summary, only about twenty percent of the fake credits were being detected at the point of purchase. The others came later, from a more extensive forensic examination of the chips. Millions of ECs were being laundered this way, as the gang accepted a twenty percent loss at the retail level.

The government of Lo'roan was offering two hundred thousand credits—hopefully, in legitimate ECs—for information regarding the operation. But then if the agent could actually bust the gang, that would earn them a million in total.

Adam leaned back in the chair and thought for a moment, trying to imagine how he would plan such a mission. First of all, he would need to ferret out sources. He was pretty good at that, seeing that, as a Human, he didn't fear moving in the seedier parts of a planet. And as far as getting information out of people, Adam had no qualms about using *enhanced interrogation* techniques as only a Human was capable. If Adam needed information out of a person, there was very little they could do to resist. Not only that, but perhaps his reputation would precede him and save him the time and effort. Give him the information … or suffer the consequences.

And best of all, Lo'roan was located only three

light-years from the passageway known as the Devil's Gate.

The Gate was an area of galactic space between six semi-stationary blackholes that had the local topography torn up into a gravitational mishmash. On the outer side, tremendous quantities of stellar gas and debris were being attracted to the singularities making travel there virtually impossible. However, because of the influence of two of the largest blackholes on each other, the space between them was relatively clear of gravitational sources, making transits possible within a narrow, tenth-of-a-light-year corridor. This was the Devil's Gate, which was derived from the Josilin-Bor phrase *Fansnon de ka Sorum*, meaning the *Gate to the Entrance of Hell*. In English—and Juirean—the name had been changed to the Devil's Gate.

On the other side of the Gate were nine inhabited worlds. Prior to the Klin invasion, they were part of the Juirean Expansion, and although never mainstream planets, they still enjoyed a relatively modern existence with outside trade and even a minor tourist industry centered on the brilliant nebulae and spiraling stars that orbited the blackholes.

After the Klin invasion failed, there were around two and a half million Klin stranded in the Milky Way. That was still a formidable fighting force, but neither they, nor the Allies, were willing to fight to the last alien. The invaders accepted the fact that their efforts were put on hold—possibly permanently—until a new portal could be opened with their universe. Adam was one of the few people in the Milky Way who knew that was not to be—ever. The Klin universe had been absorbed into another, destroying all life across two dimensions. There would be no relief for the Milky Way Klin. They were on their own.

Accepting their fate—at least temporarily—the Klin divided into six colonies so as to not pose a significant outward threat to the galaxy. The largest of these colonies moved into the Devil's Gate region and set up shop. Knowing that coming in as invaders would elicit a counter response from the Allies, the Klin came in as friends instead, offering to help the locals with marketable technology. This gave the nine worlds new products to produce and sell to the galaxy as a whole, raising the standard of living for all. The aliens then spread themselves among the populace, making it more difficult for an attacking force to weed them out without significant collateral damage. Most, however, settled on the planet Arancus.

And this was where the bank was located.

Adam nodded approvingly. Yes, this counterfeiting job would do nicely. He'd be doing something he didn't normally do with a new puzzle to solve. Hell, he may even bust the perpetrators and make an extra million—oh, wait. Tidus wouldn't let him keep it. He shrugged. Oh well, at least he'd get to bust a few alien heads along the way. That was always the highlight of Adam's day.

Tidus read over the data-listing with a deep frown on his long forehead.

"Seriously? A counterfeiting operation? How is this going to make us credits—unless we print the credits ourselves?"

"All I need to do is find where they are and turn the information over to the authorities. It'll be a piece of cake."

Tidus shook his head. "Not so fast. The locals have been stymied; what makes you think you can do any better?"

Adam grinned and held his hands out in front of him, like The Fonz. "Hey, I'm the *Human*. Haven't you read my press releases? I can do anything."

"Anything ... except get paid for a job."

Adam grimaced. He'd walked into that one.

"Let's face it, Tidus, if I find out where they are, you know I'm going to go in and bust them. And these are counterfeiters. They ain't no shooting army. As I said, a piece of cake."

Tidus then leaned in closer to his screen. "And I suppose you missed this little detail."

"What detail?"

"About the Clan of the Hood."

Adam looked at his datapad. He *had* missed that part. But there it was, as almost a side note. *'The operation is believed to be sponsored by the Clan of the Hood.'*

"It's just a rumor."

Tidus stared at Adam. "You've heard of Halon Grasnic?"

Adam nodded. He knew where this was going.

"I worked with him at Priority Acquisitions. One of the best. He went after the Clan about a year ago and was never heard from again. And there have been four or five others. All top-notch mercs. If the Clan is involved, then this may not be as simple as you think."

"It says they *may* be the sponsors. I wouldn't be going after the Clan itself."

"You could still piss them off if you interfere with one of their operations."

Adam smiled wryly. "Are you afraid of the Clan?"

"Damn right I am!" Tidus exclaimed. "They're a legend, ghosts that no one has ever identified. And supposedly, there's only a handful of them, but they still pull off some of the most spectacular crimes in the galaxy, and always high cash operations, banks, depositories and the like. It would make sense that they also do counterfeiting. These assholes are money hungry."

"Relax, Tidus. I'm going there primarily for information. I get it, turn it over to the locals, and then get paid. I don't need to do anything more than that unless I want to."

Tidus was still shaking his head.

"No, I can't allow it. Besides, it's all the way to the Gate. That's too far away."

Adam firmed his jaw. This was going to take a little more convincing than he thought. "Remember, Tidus, when you asked me to come work at Starfire you said I could pick and choose my own jobs."

"That was before you started losing money rather than making it."

"Fair enough, but that's only been the past few jobs. Before that, I've made you millions. And not only that, but you've been using my reputation to enhance the credibility of your company for years. Having *The Human* on your payroll probably means an extra ten percent on all your other jobs, and you know it. I know I've screwed up recently, but you have to trust me on this one. I can make short work of it."

Tidus cast his beady golden eyes on Adam. "Why do I get the feeling like I'm being played? What aren't you telling me?"

Adam anticipated the question. It was time to be honest … to a point. "I'm bored," Adam breathed. "There it is … I'm bored."

"Explain."

"You, more than most, know what I mean. I'm a lot older than I look—something like thirty years older

—and I'm tired of doing the same old thing; chase down some fugitive, bust some heads and then get paid. That's why I'm more into mercenary work these days. It's more of a challenge. And now I'd have a chance to play cop on some alien planet, investigating a real crime rather than chasing after someone we already know is guilty. I need a mystery to solve. Closing down the operation is secondary."

Tidus continued to stare at Adam. Then he sighed. "If you can bust the damn operation, please do. It will be more credits for us."

"So, I have your approval?"

"Of course not, but I'm letting you go anyway. Just remember, you owe me—and Bandors Bank. Bring back some credits … or don't come back at all. Except to return the *Arieel*. Contrary to what you believe, the ship belongs to *me*. And remember, I have a kill switch."

Adam was up off the chair and out the door before Tidus closed the quotation marks. As he raced from the building and to his transport, he made a mental note: Find and deactivate the damn kill switch. And do it as soon as possible.

6

By the time he returned to the *Arieel*, Adam was emotionally drained. He'd been through a rollercoaster, first with Oakes and his people showing up unexpectedly, then the news of the bank, and lastly, to learn that Tidus knew about the recovery fee—or lack thereof—from the beginning. And he'd only been on Tel'oran for four hours by the time he lifted off again. What else unexpected could happen?

He rendezvoused with Oakes' ship thirty minutes later and after giving the team the rundown on the counterfeiting job on Lo'roan, they set off in tandem out from the system, setting a course for the Devil's Gate. As it was with all space travel, it was a matter of hurry up and wait, and now he had a three-week journey to their destination. That was fine; he needed time to plan dual missions: the bank job and how to track down the counterfeiting ring.

But for the moment, he relished the smoothing quiet of gravity-well travel, along with the comforting familiarity of the *Arieel*'s hums and vibration. He slumped back in the pilot's seat, crossed his arms, and prepared to take a welcome nap. He needed the rest—

"Surprise!"

If the internal gravity aboard the *Arieel* had been set at Juirean Standard rather than Earth Standard, Adam's Human muscles would have sent him crashing into the cockpit's low-slung ceiling as he jumped. Instead, his heart was in his throat and his arms flailing as he tumbled off the chair and to the grated metal deck. He crawled on his hands and knees around the command console and then popped his head up, looking aft toward the source of the unexpected sound. He wasn't normally this skittish, but the last thing he expected was the presence of another person, aboard his ship, and in space.

He was in even more shock when he saw the sensual form of a near-naked Callie Morrison standing in the doorway, one arm stretched seductively above her head and along the door frame, with the other resting on a shapely hip. Her brilliant red hair was curled and fell enticingly past her shoulders, with a fair amount of it channeled into her amble cleavage, pointing the way.

"Sorry, did I startle you?" Callie blinked, her pale skin blushing from embarrassment. "I guess I did."

"No shit, Callie! What did you expect?" Adam remained on his knees, peering over the console. "What the hell are you doing here?"

Adam didn't need any more surprises. He'd met his quota for the day, hell, for the month.

Callie covered her chest with her arms, suddenly feeling exposed. "I had a problem with the *Angel* and needed to make repairs. Tel'oran was the closest planet. I came to see you—to surprise you. I fell asleep while waiting for you to get back. And then you took off without any warning."

"How did you get aboard? I'm sure I locked the door this time."

Callie smiled sheepishly. "You know me. I have certain skills. Lockpicking is one of them. Along with safecracking, security systems and a lot more. I'm a girl of many talents. After all, I robbed Bandors Bank. Not too many people could do that."

Adam shrugged. She had a point. But it also meant he needed a different type of lock, and not one that could be so easily picked.

"So, where are you going in such a hurry?" Callie asked. "Didn't you just get back to Tel'oran?"

Adam came over and took her in his arms, embarrassed by his initial reaction. They hugged and shared a kiss, something quick and sweet. Once the awkwardness vanished, there would be time for more passion.

"You're right, but something new came up and I'm off on another assignment."

"So, Tidus didn't fire you?"

Adam shook his head. "You can say I'm on probation."

"Is that how it works with your company; no rest for the wicked, with one job after another?"

The pair walked back to the common room before Callie ducked into the stateroom and grabbed her shirt. Although they'd been intimate before, Adam could tell she didn't feel comfortable sitting in just her panties and bra unless there was a reciprocal response from him. At the moment, he was too distracted to think about anything other than the weirdness of the day. But the more he studied her lithe and athletic body, the more his focus was changing.

"About Tidus, that bastard," Adam began. "I learned that he knew all about the shortage and the hundred kay from the beginning, hell, even before I did. The bank called him after we returned the money. He's known all along but didn't say anything."

"Why did he do that?"

"To see if I would tell him first."

Callie pursed her lips. "Oh … oops."

"Yeah, oops. I've really let him down, and so I took a quick job to make it up to him."

"That makes sense. So, what's the job?"

Immediately, alarms went off in Adam's head. He wasn't sure why, except that he didn't believe in coincidences. Another was the fact that Callie Morrison was a professional con-artist with the morals of a honey badger. Although she was hotter than hell, and had helped him out when it counted, if it hadn't been for her in the first place, he wouldn't have been shot, tossed over a cliff and left for dead. And that was just the beginning of their brief fling together. Adam enjoyed her company, but he didn't trust her any farther than he could throw her.

"It's just a little detective work—information only—not even a recovery."

Callie laughed. "*The Human* isn't assigned *little* detective work. You're a rockstar. You only get the choice assignments."

Adam smirked. "If you only knew how wrong that statement is. But if you insist, it's a counterfeiting ring out on a planet called Lo'roan. The authorities want to find out who they are. All I need to do is find out and the Feds will do the rest."

Callie frowned. "I know Lo'roan; it's a real shithole. There's one big, massive city there called Durin. Even so, the job does seem to be a little below your paygrade."

"I'm doing it just to pay back Tidus. It turns out he had to co-sign for the hundred kay to the bank."

Now Callie's eyes lit up and she burst into laughter. "No shit? That's funny. And no wonder you're off on such a lame assignment. I'm sure he's going to ride your ass until you pay back the bank. My dad co-signed for my first car. He made me make double payments until it was paid off because—" she used finger quotes and a lower voice—"because my name's on the damn loan, too."

"Then you know why I'm doing this."

Adam had reached the stage where he could no longer ignore the ample charms of the near-naked Callie Morrison. "Let me turn the ship around and put it on autopilot. Then I'll be ready for that surprise you have for me." He grinned wickedly. "After a little sex among the stars, I'll take you back to Tel'oran."

"There's no need to take me back. I wouldn't mind a little vacation, not after the year I've had. Besides, I can help; I know a lot of people in Durin, and just the kind who might know about counterfeiters. Let me help—for no charge. After all, I feel partially responsible for you owing the bank in the first place."

Adam's mind was a jumble. The Lo'roan job was just a diversion, but he still needed to show results before the team could head through the Gate and the General's confidential source. And they needed the *Arieel* to get into Klin-controlled space. Having someone like Callie on his side could speed up the process. But then how could he and the others plan the Klin bank job with Callie aboard?

Then Adam thought, *What's half-a-billion divided by five?*

He winked. "Go into my stateroom and get ready," he said as he headed for the cockpit. "I have to make a quick link. Give me ten minutes."

Callie had been holding the blouse against her chest, having never put it on. Now she let it drop to the floor. "Ten minutes? I'm not sure I can wait that long." She reached behind her back and unfastened the bra strap. Then she stood up and waved her hands across her body. "What could be more important than this? Make it five minutes, stud."

Adam raced to the cockpit as Callie slipped into his stateroom. He had to let the team know what was happening and now he had an incentive to talk fast. Really fast.

Callie was impressed with herself. If ever she had put on an Academy Award winning performance, it was when Adam linked with the other ship and put the team on the screen. She marveled at what suckers the men were for a pretty face, blue eyes and flaming red hair. At first, they didn't even want to talk to her. But after Adam spent only a few minutes explaining who she was and how she could help, he put her on the screen. That was all it took.

Callie acted stunned by the news of the bank, but by then, she could sense the men's eyes upon her and the not-so-subtle change of attitude. It was obvious the three males had been in space long enough to where the sight of a Human woman set off a plethora of primal instincts. She played on that.

Adam did his part, as well, by filling in what he knew of her background. He even threw in a reference to her safecracking and security system skills, something she had only recently told him about, even as it was mostly fake. She knew bank accounting computer systems, which was how she stole the original twenty-five million from Bandors Bank. But other than that, she only learned skills as needed, and she'd never broken into a bank vault before. But that didn't stop her from embellishing her resume.

In the end, it wasn't only Adam who invited her along for the bank caper, it was all of them, especially the cute young one named Jay Williford. He was virtually salivating looking at her through the screen. And then there was the dark-haired brooding one whose black eyes locked with hers and held them. His name was Mike Hannon. Hell, even the square-jawed, silver-fox of an aging army officer—Todd Oakes—was a hunk. Callie felt herself go flush at the prospects of working not only with Humans again, but with four absolute hunks. Damn her good luck!

With her mission to join the team a smashing success, Callie settled down for the remainder of the trip to Lo'roan, contributing the best she could to the planning of both missions. She *did* know people in the ungodly large and sprawling metropolis of Durin; she hoped she had enough B.S. left in her to fake the rest of her story. So far in her career, her bullshit skills had been her ace in the hole. And having a nice ass didn't hurt, either.

7

The *Arieel* and General Oakes' ship—a clunky surplus destroyer from the Human space fleet called the *USF Farragut*—were in a joined gravity-well using the warship's focusing rings to generate the singularity. This allowed an umbilical tube to be run between the vessels for access to both ships while still in a well. Interaction between the co-conspirators was essential as the operation to rob the Klin bank was planned. The destroyer was much larger than the *Arieel* so the team spent most of the time aboard the vessel.

Adam had three datapads and a whiteboard spread out on the plot table on the bridge, with a dozen archaic sheets of real paper scattered about, as well, all with notes he'd been making about various plans he was working on. The other four Humans were now hunched over the mess, shuffling between versions, wearing frowns and adding their two cents to everything Adam came up with.

Finally, General Oakes tossed a small stack of papers onto the counter and stepped back.

"This is ridiculous. None of this is any good without more intelligence."

"I've been telling you that for the past two weeks," Adam said with exasperation. "We need to get the details of the actual layout of the building, along with the security system at the bank."

"No one said it would be easy," Oakes said in his defense. It was Oakes—in his capacity as a retired general working for the Defense Intelligence Department on Earth—who first learned of the energy credits being held in the Klin bank. It was he who put all this in motion, which, as Adam was learning, was based mostly on rumor and guesswork. Even so, the truth of the matter was hardly in dispute; the Klin had energy credits and they needed a lot of them to buy supplies for their people. But how much and where they were kept came mainly from reports passed down from only a few eyewitnesses, along with a lot of secondhand rumors.

The primary eyewitness source came from a Lap'polin living on the planet Josilin-Bor just inside the Devil's Gate. He was an electronics expert who worked on most of the planets within the region and had personally worked on the vault mechanisms. He'd seen the security crates. But if the reports could be believed, he was the only one of the sources who had actually been in the bank. The rest were other technicians or merchants who spoke of transactions they'd done with the Klin and how they'd been paid.

But still, the Lap'polin said he had more information for the Humans—including the layout of the bank building, complete with schematics, but would only give it to them once they paid him his fee ... and paid it in person.

Adam had only met one other Lap'polin. It was on Adam's adopted second homeworld of Navarus, and the creature had been his real estate agent when Adam bought the building that would later be converted into *Capt. Cain's Bar & Grill*. His name was Lion/El, and the purple skinned, four-armed creature had gone on to become the president of the planet, if only temporarily. Adam didn't know what became of the alien during the Klin occupation of Navarus, but knowing him, he probably came out just fine. He was a smooth operator first and foremost, able to shake your hand with one of his while using the other three to skillfully pick your pockets. He would survive.

If the rest of the race was like Lion/El, then Adam didn't know how much stock he could put on what the informant had to tell them about the bank. And besides that, he wanted twenty-five thousand ECs for the information.

Prior to leaving Tel'oran, Adam drained his account of all except five thousand credits, and then pooling his money with that from the rest of the team, they had one hundred nine thousand credits as operating capital. And twenty-five of that had to go to the electrician. That didn't leave a lot. And to top that, Adam still had a mission to carry out before they could make the move into the Devil's Gate. It would be tight.

Adam also spent part of the time during the trip to Lo'roan researching the counterfeiting operation and the Clan of the Hood. Lo'roan was one of those near-water worlds with only one major land mass along with the infamous city of Durin that held almost seventy percent of the planet's population. Adam had to double check the numbers. Durin was a massive settlement of almost one hundred ninety million people. Adam had never seen a city with that many people; in fact, never even heard of one that huge. But in a way, it would make his job of tracking down the counterfeiters that much easier because all their illegal activities took place within a single city.

Lo'roan—and Durin specifically—was the funnel through which all commerce flowed into the Gate. Unfortunately, the informant they needed to meet was located on the other side, on Josilin-Bor—the homeworld of the Lap'polin. Since the General's ship wouldn't be allowed through the Gate, the rest of the team couldn't forge ahead with the bank job while Adam was on Lo'roan chasing down the counterfeiters. It would have to be one mission at a time. Fortunately, this also meant Adam had a ready and willing team of four additional Humans to help him with his task, and with Callie's contacts being his ace in the hole. Besides, if one *Human* was a force to be reckoned with, five was a literal tsunami of alien badassness.

From space, the planet Lo'roan was the most unusual place Adam had ever seen. That was because it was nighttime in Durin. The lights of a city that huge merged together to form a solid splash of light that covered half of the dark side, turning the black ball into a flashlight on a planetary scale. A single moon orbited the planet and the radiance from Durin reflected off the surface over two hundred thousand miles away. The scene was both beautiful and eerie.

Tidus had already contacted the Lo'roan government and made arrangements for Adam to be deputized to carry out the investigation. That was part of the contract that was signed. Adam would be operating as an agent of the government while on the planet. A brief summary of implied powers was sent over and Adam grimaced as he read them. He liked the idea of working under official cover; what he didn't like were some of the restrictions placed on his activities. It was almost as if the authorities on Lo'roan were protecting the rights of their citizens against excessive force, something that was also common on Earth. Adam smirked. He really didn't have a problem with that; he just wasn't used to such restrictions working in the wild and wooly Milky Way. Usually anything went. But on Lo'roan, he'd have to watch his manners.

It was decided that Adam and Callie would check in at police headquarters while the other three Humans watched their back. If the Clan of the Hood really was involved, then it paid to have backup. Besides, having five Humans walking down the street together was bound to attract too much attention. Even on Lo'roan, they'd heard of Humans. Most of the galaxy had.

The two starships were assigned landing space at one of the nineteen hundred spaceports servicing the city-state, this one closest to the government facilities. The ride to the surface was awe inspiring. The city went on and on; a confusing mixture of skyscrapers and tenements, high-brow neighborhoods and ghettos. From the sky, it looked as if the planet was alive, as countless roadways, clogged with horrific traffic, pulsed like veins in a body. It was hypnotic.

It also smelled to high heaven.

Even through the scent of the exhaust gasses, the stench of Durin permeated the hulls of the ships, becoming nearly intolerable by the time they landed.

"Do we wear masks here?" Jay Williford asked through the comm. He was aboard the *Farragut* with Mike and Todd, while Callie and Adam were in the *Arieel*.

"You'll get used to it," Callie said with a grin. "Besides, masks won't help. This is what you get when you cram almost two hundred million aliens into a closed space. And another thing, there's no way to tell who's indigenous and who isn't. The native population was overwhelmed thousands of years ago to the point where no one knows who's original and who's an outsider. And nobody cares. Durin exists to funnel every imaginable item to and from the Gate. It's all about the credits here. Everything is for sale, even life and death."

Jay elbowed Mike Hannon on the screen. "Sounds like your kind of place."

Mike scowled at the young man. "I don't know why you guys keep talking like I'm this great alien assassin. I did it for a while, that's all. It wasn't like it was my permanent occupation. In fact, after that time on

Navarus with Adam and the Juirean, I haven't done another hit."

Callie looked at Adam. "Juirean? Does he mean Tidus?"

"Nah, it was another one. The guy next in line to be the Juirean Elder."

"The Elder! The leader of the Expansion?" She looked at Mike through the screen. "You killed the Juirean Elder?"

"He wasn't the Elder yet." Mike shrugged. "I guess he never did become the Elder."

"Yeah, because you killed him," the general said acidly. "And almost started another Human-Juirean war."

"That's what they wanted to happen," Mike said in his defense. "If you recall, we stopped it from spiraling out of control."

Callie was staring at Mike, a silly grin on her face. "Still, I think that's hot. You killed a guy who could have ruled a galaxy."

Mike smiled nervously. "Hey, I was young; I needed the money."

Everyone laughed, except Adam. "Okay, knock it off. Let's concentrate on the mission at hand. Mike and Jay, you go and rent us a couple of transports. I have a bag of tracking devices we all need to wear. This place is too big for us to get separated. Then Callie and I will go check in at the police station. After that, she has a meeting set with a fence she knows; someone she's done business with before. It's a good place to start."

The transport smelled like crap—literally—which Adam assumed had to be pervasive to be detected within the overall stench of the city. Callie was right; you can't pack this many aliens into a single city and expect it to smell like a summer breeze. As they were landing, Adam noticed the ring of small hills surrounding Durin, thinking how they defined the border of the community. On closer examination, they were mountains of trash towering about a thousand feet high. An army of tractors moved up and down the mounds, adding another foot or two to the elevation every day. On more civilized worlds, trash was either burned or infused with a type of glue that turned it into building materials. They may still do that in Durin, but the sheer volume of refuse overwhelmed the system. And the city was still growing. This many people produced even more people to the tune of half a million new residents a day simply from births. Even the deaths—which were prodigious—couldn't temper the population growth. Durin was some dystopian writer's worst nightmare.

Adam and Callie relied on GPS to guide them to the main police station for the city/planet since it was impossible to follow the roads on their own. Adam tested the comms, making sure both elements of the team could communicate with each other and that his backup didn't get lost.

Miles before they reached their destination, the roads began to be filled with official vehicles numbering in the thousands. A population this large required a concomitant police force to maintain even a semblance of law and order. Adam wouldn't be surprised to learn that the police force for Durin was larger than most planet's active military.

After taking far too long to find the proper building and then office, an already exhausted and frustrated Adam Cain and Callie Morrison finally entered the department that would issue them their operating papers. The aliens—a variety of them—stared mockingly at the Humans, knowing why they were there. An inside joke was circulating that made Adam think the police force wasn't taking the counterfeiters seriously.

Eventually, an older officer wearing a circle with two hashmarks on his shoulder guided them into his office. Two subordinates followed.

"We received the operating agreement from your supervisor; it is all standard material," the creature said seemingly bored. "We have transmitted the ratified contract to Tel'oran." He looked at Callie. "The agreement is for only one agent."

"I understand," Adam said. "She is an advisor only. I'm the one to be deputized."

All three aliens snickered.

"Is there a problem?" Adam asked.

"No problem," said the lead officer. "It is just that deputization is a glorification of the status you are being granted." He handed Adam a data chip that was scanned across his pad to download the information. "This is a list of authorizations and restrictions on your status. Study them carefully. Too often independents, such as yourself, overstep their boundaries and problems occur." His grey eyes studied Callie and then Adam. "You are Humans; I recognize the species. In truth, *you* are the agent known as *The Human*, signifying an elevated level of competence, I am to assume. With experience, you should already be aware of these restrictions. I must inform you that you will be held accountable for your actions. You are here for an assignment; that is all. You are not an official member of the Durin Security Force and are not to represent yourself as one."

"Then why give me the status at all?" Adam had encountered self-righteous assholes like this before and he was growing impatient.

"A formality, to protect the government against rogue elements operating without sanction. At least this way, we will have some control over your actions."

"You're deputizing me … so you can have control of me?"

The alien's eyes grew wide. "That is an accurate reading; I am impressed. Most of your kind never grasp the concept until it is too late."

The officer entered data into his computer as the other two agents began chatting among themselves, seemingly dismissing the pair of Humans.

"Don't we get a badge or something?" Adam asked.

The aliens laughed, and then the leader pressed back in his chair and stretched out a grin, careful not to expose his teeth in a death challenge.

"Badge?" He looked at the other two agents and then back to Adam. "You do not need a badge! I have entered your status; all Security Force members can check your status if they wish. And your status does *not* give you permission to violate any Durin law, to exert authority over citizens or to enter property without expressed permission."

"How are we to find the counterfeiters if you're tying our hands? I thought you wanted these guys caught and their operation shut down."

"Politicians and bankers have pressed the issue, Human. The operation you speak of is non-violent and in a way, beneficial to the economy of Durin. The credits may be artificial, but is not every official currency? I have been instructed to grant you permission to work within the city, but I do not have to assist.

There is a reward offered at various stages of the operation; I suggest you earn it."

The two other agents in the room were in awe of their articulate supervisor. They snickered as Adam and Callie left the office for the long hike through the maze of buildings back to their transport. They would get no support from the locals; in fact, Adam was kicking himself for even reporting in. Now, he was on their radar, and it was apparent they'd be watching him closer than they were watching the criminals.

8

"Did you get all that?" Adam said through the micro-comm. It was a strip of flesh-colored material behind his ear that an alien would have trouble detecting unless they were intimate with Human physiology.

"Rude bastard, wasn't he?" General Oakes commented. "I would hazard a guess he knows exactly who these counterfeiters are and where they're located. Most of these slum police forces are on the take; most just aren't so blatant about it."

"Roger that," Adam said. "Stay close. According to the satellite feed, we're heading into a dilapidated part of town."

"What part isn't dilapidated?" Jay Williford asked. "This has to be the worst shithole I've ever been in. And I've been to Detroit."

Callie was strangely quiet as Adam drove them into a congested maze of cockeyed streets and around minefields of trash, abandoned vehicles and crumbling buildings, just the type of place one would expect to find a major criminal operation. She wouldn't meet his eyes as they reached the address and left the transport, making sure to lock it the car. It probably wouldn't make a difference, but at least he tried. The team pulled to the curb a block down the street and in view of the car. If anyone tried to tamper with it, they'd have three Humans to deal with.

A hundred eyes were on them, from the street, windows and doorways. Adam felt like a gazelle running the gauntlet through a pride of lions. It was expected. He'd been through this hundreds of times before; in fact, at another time he would have invited a confrontation. Weak boned aliens were fun to beat on.

Callie led them to a doorway and entered without knocking. Although she was acting strange, she still carried herself with confidence. Probably as much as Adam, she was used to places like this.

The interior was dark and humid, with peeling paint on the walls, broken bottles on the floor and discarded furniture. It was almost a stereotype, setting Adam on edge.

Two seemingly inert bums suddenly came alive and

stood up, taking up guard positions on either side of an interior door. Callie stepped up to them.

"We're here to see Dann Ma'ddan. He's expecting us."

One of the aliens ducked inside the room while the other held a hand under a filthy trench coat where he undoubtedly had a hidden weapon. Adam and Callie were armed, just not overtly. They carried compact laser weapons in their pockets which were great for Close Quarters Combat. They also had their comms active with the remainder of the team.

The impossibly skinny alien came out of the room and left the door open. He nodded with a narrow head. Callie took the lead.

As expected, the room was clear and better decorated, betraying the illusion given off by the rundown neighborhood and building's foyer. A plump, yellow-skinned alien sat at a desk, his hand held below the tabletop, a hidden gun at the ready just in case. He had an extremely long neck, a powerful lower body and a bell-shaped figure. Round black eyes stared unblinking at the Humans.

"I'm Callie Morrison, I was referred to you by Sanders Bilk. He said you are a dealer in contraband, as well as information."

Adam cast a sideways glance at Callie. She told him she'd worked with the fence before. It was now apparent this was the first time they'd met. That didn't help Adam with his trust issues.

Adam's eyes widened and he took a half step back when suddenly a watermelon size bubble popped out of the alien's neck. It was thin and threaded with veins. Slowly, the bubble began to deflate and the alien started to speak.

"Message I received. Said you need information. I facilitate many things. Information one. Explain your need."

The voice tapered off as the neck returned to normal.

"We are looking for information regarding a group making fake energy credits. From what we can tell, they may be well known to some."

The creature nodded, then his neck bubbled out again.

"Is dangerous, the information you seek. And expensive. Are you prepared to pay? Only cause to speak is because of Sanders. The party you seek protected."

"We will pay five thousand credits for information as to the location."

Adam and Callie hadn't discussed this before, although she knew how much money the team had in operating capital.

The fence stared at the Humans, his eyes never

blinking, his emotions impossible to read. His shoulders began to vibrate.

"Not enough for location but will refer to another for price."

"So, you know where they are?" Adam asked. If it was a matter of price, he might consider paying more if it would speed up the hunt.

Bubble-neck recoiled at Adam's strong, male voice. He was easily eight feet tall, but Adam got the impression he wasn't the physical type. Again the skin billowed, and then like a bagpipe, began to deflate.

"Five thousand and I call another to take you to location. I may know location; I may not. Prefer to remain distinct."

Adam interpreted distinct to mean staying at arm's length from the counterfeiters. He had to operate in the underworld of Durin. He couldn't be ratting on his fellow criminals and expect to stay in business, or alive. Especially if there was a chance the Clan of the Hood was involved.

Adam was again kicking himself for registering with the authorities. If not, he might have beat the information out of the fence. Instead, he behaved himself and pulled out a stack of energy chips, counting out five thousand credits worth. Ma'dann took them and then discretely spoke in a communicator, pumping his throat up in a rhythmic dance that Adam found fascinating. Aliens came in such wonderous varieties, prompting Adam to question how easy would it be to pop Ma'dann's throat bubble? He was tempted to poke at it when the alien spoke to the Humans again.

"In area. Meet outside. Ten standard minutes. Wait there. Not here."

Adam was all for that. The stench was nearly unbearable, and Ma'dann's breath smelled like fish. Rotting fish. Both he and Callie took several deep breaths out on the street, amazed that they would reach a point where polluted outside air was preferable to inside air. The sooner they got off Lo'roan, the better.

"I thought you said you'd worked with bubble-throat before?" Adam asked Callie as they waited on the street for the second contact.

"I said I've heard of him."

"That's not what you said," Adam countered. Neither of the Humans looked at each other; instead their eyes darted over the myriad of beings along the street. Looks were deceiving, just as had been the two guards inside the building. Ma'dann could have an army of derelicts guarding his building.

"Just trying to make myself more important," Callie admitted. "I'm the new player in the game. I wanted to make an impression. It got us another contact. And we're still alive, so no harm done."

Adam understood where she was coming from. Even still, she had lied to him and the team. Trust was paramount in a combat squad; she should know that. She'd been Marine Force Recon back on Earth—if she had been telling the truth about that.

Their attention was drawn to a vehicle coming down the road toward them. It passed Hannon and the others and began to slow. What set it apart from all the others on the street was how clean it was. It was an impressive stretch version of the standard electric vehicle found on every civilized world in the galaxy, black in color and with heavily tinted windows. It was midday on Lo'roan, but even still, it was impossible to see inside. Adam instinctively gripped the laser pistol in his pocket.

"Everybody on alert," he whispered.

"We're on it," Mike answered.

The limo stopped at the curb and the window moved down. A dark figure moved inside, a figure in a hood!

Suddenly, a dozen of the vagrants on the street jumped to their feet revealing flash weapons. All were pointed at the two Humans.

"Hold!" Adam said softly through his comm. "Let's see how this plays out. There's a dude in a hood inside the car."

"The Clan?" Mike asked.

"A good bet."

"You will accompany me," said the hooded figure. "Do not resist. We will not hesitate to kill you."

There were two doors in the back, and the rear door now opened as half a dozen aliens searched them thoroughly, removing the laser weapons before shoving them inside the vehicle. Two burly beasts with MKs were in the next forward seat. They were looking back at the Humans, eyes alert with the intensity of professionals. The hooded figure was seated next to the right window. Call it professional curiosity but Adam was anxious to study a member of the secretive Clan of the Hood. These guys were known across the galaxy, yet no one knew who they were. Adam was about to find out.

The car took off. The Humans could clearly see out the windows although they were masked to the inside. The transport barreled down the road, not stopping at corners or yielding to surrounding traffic. Everyone in this part of Durin recognized the vehicle and gave it the right of way.

Mr. Hood was quiet and stoic during the drive, not looking back at his guests. Still, Adam was able to study the garment. It was grey and appeared to be made of metal not fabric. It could be both a cloak and a shield. In the brief moment Adam had a look toward the face, all he saw was a second shroud, this one made of black mesh disguising the beast's identity, even under the hood. Considering the depth of the seats and comparative size of the guards looking back at the Humans, Adam estimated the Clan member was about seven and a half feet tall, typical alien height.

Callie and Adam shared a look, at which time, Callie looked past Adam and out the window and opened her eyes wide. Then she grimaced. Adam was pretty sure he knew what she was getting at. He was thinking the same thing. They could see out the window … and they hadn't been blindfolded. That meant the Clan didn't care what they heard or saw; they weren't going to live long enough to tell the tale.

"So, where are we going?" Adam asked. "And shouldn't we talk credits before you take us wherever you're taking us? Maybe your price will be too high, in which case you can let us off here."

Mr. Hood said nothing and kept staring ahead, not even turning his head to look out the window.

But Adam and Callie *were* permitted to do some sightseeing, taking in the varied scenery of Durin—for what good it would do them. They studied the passing landscape, which was the stereotypical ghetto that went on for miles. But then things began to change.

They'd been traveling for an hour and were now in a business district, complete with buildings sporting polished stone walls and banks of windows, along with greenbelt areas where employees were enjoying the afternoon sunshine. Adam didn't know there were such nice areas of Durin but figured that out of a population this large and diverse there had to be better parts of town.

"Mike here," came a voice in Adam's ear. "Just checking in. We're about six or seven car lengths behind you. It's not that hard to do. The car you're in is like following an ambulance through traffic. We're heading west toward the hills, and not the trash hills. The satellite still shows about two hours of travel time to get out of the city if we're going that far. This is a big ass place."

Adam cleared his throat, disguising a 'thanks' within it. He was wondering if the team was still following. If not, then he and Callie would have to take matters into their own hands. He wasn't about to go quietly into the night. Adam Cain never did.

Although Adam didn't know where they were going, the fact that Mike said it would take two hours to get out of town told him that was where they were headed as the hours ticked off. Eventually, the topography changed and the car entered an impressive neighborhood dotted with estates nestled fairly close to each other on the limited flat land. Durin had its haves and have nots, and the Clan evidently liked the finer things in life.

The car pulled into a short driveway that wound around the front of a three-story home constructed of native stone. Six other vehicles were scattered around the driveway and guards meandered about with weapons concealed. This may be the home of a galaxy-wide gangster, but he didn't want the neighbors to know about it, although they probably already suspected.

Adam and Callie were escorted from the car and into the building. They were both experienced enough not to be overwhelmed by the grandeur of the residence; instead, they surveyed the room for ingress and egress and covering points.

They moved along a side hallway and then down a long stairway to a huge underground work area. Here there were a dozen heavy machines, cranking away, their sound hidden from the street by the depth of the chamber.

It was the hub of the counterfeiting operation and not just a residence. A couple of dozen people were hard at work, laboring at presses and with stacks of plastic chips—some printed, some not—placed upon steel worktables. The Humans continued to follow the Clan member through the workspace and into a quieter room, almost a living room set up with couches and chairs. A pale creature in a white suit sat on an equally white couch, an intoxicant in his hand and looking satisfied as he watched the Humans brought before him.

His head was narrow and the eyes almond shaped. A set of short, curving horns grew out from his temples giving him the look of a devil. In fact, a lot of alien species had horns, and even a few with tails. In reality, there were a lot of devil races scattered throughout the cosmos.

Mr. Hood ignored the being on the couch, walking past him and then sat in a throne-like chair at the far end of the room. It was almost too far away from which to carry on a conversation.

Then Adam noticed the two police officers from the supervisor's office seated in another section of the room. They eyed Adam and Callie with humor, thinking their presence here was some great revelation to the Humans, but Adam had already figured out the security force was deep in the pockets of the Clan. It was no surprise to see them here.

"Welcome, intrepid adventurers," said the creature in white, his voice smooth and with a sing-song cadence, even when run through Adam's universal translation device embedded behind his right ear. Adam wanted to tell the alien that this was too much white for one room, and that his skin tone did not look good in it. It made him appear sickly. But Adam didn't tell him. Instead, he was thinking how much pressure it would take to snap the alien's neck.

"I have been informed that you came all the way to Lo'roan to discover my secret operation. Now that you have, what do you think? Impressive, is it not? I know it is not what you expected, to find it here of all places. But when one is producing millions in counterfeit energy credits, why not live in luxury, paid for by the illusionary credits? It is better than where the disgusting creature Dann Ma'dann resides. I wanted you to see the contrast so you could better appreciate what I have accomplished."

"You mean what the Clan of the Hood has accomplished," Adam said, testing the waters on who this person was and his relationship with the mysterious Clan.

A cloud came over the confident face of the pale alien and he gave a furtive glance to the Clan member seated twenty feet away.

"Our relationship is one of mutual benefit. The Clan supports us, and in turn, we pay them a substantial dividend." The alien waved an impatient hand. "But you are not here to discuss the Clan of the Hood. You are here to close down my operation." The grin returned to the alien's face.

"I am Qallen Laznick and I manage this facility. I must admit that the only reason you are here is because of your reputation. Normally, we dispatch agents as soon as they arrive." Qallen appeared to gnash his teeth. "The only reason there is still a bounty is because of a rival with influence in part of the Assembly. She wishes to close me down by offering the reward. Otherwise, on Lo'roan, our indiscretions are rarely advertised beyond the planet." He looked at Callie. "However, when I heard that *The Human* was to join in the long list of bounty agents seeking to track me down, I was curious to meet you firsthand. What I was not expecting is two Humans! That is delightful. As you can tell, I am old enough to remember a time when Humans were much more dominant within the galaxy, although your kind were never prevalent in the neighborhood of the Devil's Gate. Even so, the stories of your species' exploits is legend. So, before I kill you, I wanted to have the opportunity to meet Humans in the flesh. Please do not be insulted, but you are much smaller than I imagined. I am somewhat disappointed."

Adam looked again at Mr. Hood. "So am I. When I heard that the Clan was sponsoring the operation, I expected it to be much larger. Instead, you run it out of the basement in a house. Not that impressive. I guess the reputation of the Clan is mostly fable, the product of an effective public relations department if I had to guess."

The silent and stoic Mr. Hood hesitated for a moment before rising to his feet and stepping over to

Adam. With lightning quick reflexes, he delivered a surprisingly powerful backhand to Adam's head that jarred his senses and sent him toppling to the floor. Even with Adam's cloning-enhanced tolerance of pain, the hit was incredible. And not only that, but the alien didn't appear any worse for wear. Normally, if Adam was hit that hard it would shatter the hand of his attacker. Not with this creature.

As Adam groggily retook his chair, Mr. Hood returned to his seat, staring at Adam through the black abyss of his cloak.

Qallen didn't appear as entertained as Adam expected him to. Instead, he looked nervous. "It is not wise to provoke the Clan, even if there is only one present. It is often a lesson learned through experience. And now that you have tested him, perhaps we can dispense with the games. I brought you here for a moment's diversion, that is all. Now, I would very much enjoy knowing that I, personally, killed not one, but two, of the mighty Humans. It will be a tale I will tell until the day I die."

"Which I'm afraid to say is not far off," Adam said defiantly, hoping—and praying—that Mike Hannon and the others were ready to come to their rescue. They had an arsenal in the trunk of the transport. Time to put it to use.

"Holy shit! He's going to kill them!" Jay Williford exclaimed a few minutes earlier. General Oakes had parked the transport down the road from the estate but with a clear view of the gated entrance. It was a damn fortress with dozens of guards. The only advantage the Humans would have was the element of surprise—plus a dozen rounds of RPG ammunition. Jay wasn't the biggest Human of the group; in fact, he was the smallest at only five foot eight. But he made up for it with his affection for things that went boom. He was at the trunk, lifting out the first RPG and handing it to Mike. Oakes had six heavy M88 assault rifles and bags of ammunition draped over his broad shoulders as the team moved toward the entrance to the estate.

"We're on our way," Jay said in a panic through the comm. Adam had just been smacked by the Clan member. He and Callie were under the building somewhere, and there was an army of guards to work their way through to get to them. "Sorry, but the two of you are going to have to help yourselves for a few minutes. We're coming in, but we'll have to blast our way through."

Adam didn't answer but the team could hear the alien speaking, meaning Adam and Callie were still alive. But now this Qallen creature was talking about killing them himself. That could happen at any time. Jay was praying Adam had a miracle up his sleeve, like he always did. But this time it could be different.

9

It wasn't Adam who had a miracle up his sleeve. It was Callie with a concussion grenade hidden in her hair. Having a mass of thick red hair on her head provided a convenient hiding place for any number of emergency items. Not only did she have the grenade, but also a pen laser. In a flash, she had them both out.

The grenade was only about the size of a golf ball, and she sent it soaring over Qallen's head toward the two police officers at the other side of the room. Simultaneously, Adam and she dove for the floor, placing their unshackled hands over their ears as the bomb went off. It wasn't much of an explosion, but against aliens, it did the trick—even on Mr. Hood.

All in all, there were nine aliens in the room and all

of them suffered the effects of the explosion in one way or the other. Mr. Hood recovered the fastest, but already Adam and Callie were sprinting for the door using their Human muscles in the light gravity of Lo'roan. A bolt launcher was pulled from under the Clan member's cloak and fired, not waiting for the weapon's targeting computer. Adam noticed this out the corner of his eyes which told him the alien's species was one of only a handful of coordinated beings with the capacity to aim and shoot without assistance. This made him extremely dangerous.

Even so, Callie and Adam were difficult moving targets to hit and they made it to the door and down the hallway toward the printing plant. Three guards came running toward the meeting room, responding to the reverberations of the explosion.

Adam was glad to see them, because Callie and he crashed into them, Callie swinging the now lit pen laser and slicing off an alien hand, while Adam lowered a shoulder and sent one guard heavily into the other. Rejuvenated from the battle, Adam pounced on the two creatures on the floor, pummeling them with powerful blows that did more than knock them out. Bone shattered and cartilage splintered, leaving the faces of the bodies unrecognizable.

"Okay, Rocky," Callie said, pulling him off the last of the aliens. "You got the win. Grab the weapons and let's go."

Adam did as he was ordered, removing two MK handguns from the aliens. Callie had a Xan-fi rifle she'd taken from her victim.

A flash bolt skirted along the wall to Adam's right, leaving a black and smoldering line in the plaster. He rolled on his back and opened up with both MK's, directed at the Clan member who had just come out of the meeting room. With impressive reactions, he ducked back inside for cover.

And that's when the whole building trembled.

Mike and Jay walked boldly up to the main gate of the estate and fired dual RPGs at the steel barrier. It offered no resistance as the explosions tore it into a thousand pieces of twisted shrapnel. Alien guards were stunned by the unexpected attack and brought their Xan-fi bolt launchers up into firing positions.

And then came the awkward pause as they waited for the targeting computers to lock onto … something. But it was too late. General Oakes had two of the M88s—one in each arm—and he opened up on full auto, sweeping the line of eight guards and cutting them literally in half from the 5.56mm NATO rounds. The sound of the weapons was ear piercing and foreign to the remaining combatants who were used to the 'poof' of flash weapons. They recoiled from the horrific sound, which gave Mike and Jay the chance to send another two grenades into their hiding places along the rim of the driveway. Stone shattered, along with alien bodies. Others were taking refuge behind the cars parked nearby. Jay sent his next round into one of them, sending the vehicle flipping over twice before landing on the guards.

"Adam, where are you?" General Oakes yelled; his words transmitted through the hands-free comm.

"In the basement, heading into the printing plant. It's under the left side of the building as you're facing it."

"We'll concentrate fire to the middle and right side. Guards are appearing like roaches; a lot more than we thought."

"Are you okay?"

"Depends on your definition of okay. But we do have enough ammo, at least for now. And thanks to that Wildman Williford, we have enough explosives to level the damn house."

"Hold off on that until we get out."

"Roger that. Just hurry."

It seemed to Adam that every alien who had been working a printing press was now armed and firing at he and Callie. Fortunately, there was enough cover in the room, along with extra weapons. As the two Humans effectively eliminated the opposition, they scooped up every weapon they could. Most had their batteries drained, but some still had a few shots in them before going dry. It was better than nothing.

Through the haze left by the coursing plasma bolts, dust and debris was raining from the ceiling as the Humans outside were laying siege to the building. Adam could hear the pops of M88 fire, punctuated by the thunderous cacophony of the RPGs going off. Although the general had said they'd concentrate on other parts of the building, that didn't seem to be holding true. It seemed that at any second, the upper floors were about to pancake down into the basement. That made the pair's flight to safety that much more urgent.

They reached the long stairway going up and Adam took the lead, leaving Callie to cover him from below. Stray flash bolts were being sent down the stairwell, which Adam did his best to evade. They were Level-2s, which although not lethal to a Human, could still cause considerable pain and physical damage. He returned fire pushing the guards back.

Then Callie was firing from behind her. Adam had no idea how far the basement ran; already he knew it extended beyond the property line and below the neighbor's house. For all Adam knew, Qallen owned that property, too. It didn't matter. But now more guards—and Mr. Hood—had caught up with them, and Callie was doing all she could to hold them at bay.

Adam had a decision to make. Either he continued up the stairs and secure the landing at the top, or he could go back down to help Callie. The other three Humans were making mincemeat of the upper floors, so Adam bounded back down, his MK releasing the last of its bolts to give Callie a little relief.

They jumped from the stairwell and into the first room they came to along the hallway. Callie slammed the door shut and looked at Adam, her eyes filled with concern.

Then her body shot forward as the door came off its hinges and flew inward landing on her unconscious body. Mr. Hood was there, having used his massive body to bash down the door. He leveled his MK at Adam, who did the same to the alien. They triggered their weapons simultaneously.

And nothing happened.

Both batteries were drained.

The combatants eyed each other momentarily, with neither taking the initiative. Normally, Adam would welcome a moment like this; one-on-one with a brittle-boned alien. But this beast was different.

The stalemate didn't last longer than a heartbeat or two before Adam and the alien came together.

Adam's superior weight and density won the first encounter, pushing the cloaked figure to the side and into the wall. Human muscles shoved him back while a left hook made its way toward his head. But the creature twisted sideways suddenly, causing Adam to miss while a powerful fist buried itself into Adam's ribcage. Air was forced from his lungs and he staggered back, coughing, giving Mr. Hood a chance to lash out with a thick leg, kicking Adam in his left kidney.

Temporarily hurt and confused, Adam retreated out of the range of the alien. Mr. Hood did not advance. Instead, he straightened up, lifted his arms and pushed back on the hood, revealing his face. Adam didn't know why he did it; either to shock Adam with his identity or to improve his fighting vision. Either way, Adam was definitely shocked by what he saw.

Not too many Humans—or anyone else in the galaxy for that matter—would have recognized the race. But Adam did. They had come close to extinction over thirty years before, and even before that, were a shadow species known only to a few—including the conniving Klin.

It was a Kracori.

That explained a lot, such as why the creature was so tough and why he could fire a weapon without the need of a targeting computer. In that regard they were nearly a match for Humans.

The Kracori came from deep within the Juddle

Nebula very close to the planet Tel'oran, in a place called the Dysion Void, and had been the surrogates the Klin were grooming for galactic domination at the time of the first Human-Juirean war. Their story was complicated, but at the moment, all Adam knew was that the scaly, grey skinned creature was a very close match to Humans. Mr. Hood wouldn't be a pushover, as he'd already demonstrated.

"A fucking Kracori," Adam said, causing the alien to recoil.

"You know?" said the beast, appearing surprised. "You would be too young to have such knowledge."

"I'm a student of history," Adam said. This wasn't the time nor the place for longer explanations. "And if you know anything of Human and Kracori interactions, you should know it won't turn out too good for you."

"I have never met a Human before, which means I have never killed one, either." He looked down at Callie's unconscious body. "I may have just remedied that. And if not, then I will start with you."

The alien took a step forward but stopped when Adam put out his hand. "Hold on a second," he began. "What the hell are you doing here? Your race is nearly extinct. Elision is a wasteland. Is the Kracori part of the Clan of the Hood? Do you wear the hoods to hide your identity?"

The Kracori shook his huge head. "You have many questions, too many."

"I'm curious."

"Yes, you are, but at the wrong time."

"Indulge me. I'm dying for answers."

"Dying is correct."

"Then what's the harm in telling me?"

"Because this is a distraction as your forces outside continue to battle. I will not give you the luxury of time."

And then he attacked again, but this time Adam knew what he was up against. It didn't mean much, it just meant that Adam had to be more careful.

He sidestepped the big alien and swept his legs. The Kracori reacted in time to avoid a fall, but Adam still used the time to swing around and land a powerful backhand to the Kracori's exposed face. The creature staggered back, spitting blood from his mouth.

Adam grinned. "See, I won't be such a pushover."

"Pushover?"

"Yeah, what you are to me."

The Kracori squinted. "Confusing remark."

"Keep thinking about it." And then Adam went on the offensive. Having already experienced the reaction speed of the alien, Adam now entered the boxing match with renewed confidence. His cloned body was firing on all cylinders by now, giving him about twenty percent more strength than even a trained warrior like himself would have. His reaction time was also quicker, and he used it to place a couple of probing jabs into the Kracori's jaw. Anger grew in the beast as he was experiencing something he'd never encountered before—someone who was faster and stronger.

The anger is what caused the creature to charge at Adam, fighting through Adam's barrage of fists to tackle him around the waist. They landed hard on the floor with Adam under the much larger body. And Kracori were much denser than average aliens, so the weight was incredible, crushing Adam's already straining lungs under the load.

And then an elbow slammed into Adam's jaw, rocking the Human and affecting his vision. Out of desperation, Adam grabbed for the alien's arms, trying to pin them against the huge body to keep them from delivering a knockout blow. It had been a long time since Adam fought an alien who could hold his own against a Human. But this was no longer a sporting contest. This was now a matter of life and death.

And that's when Adam saw the barrel of an MK-17 appear out of nowhere to press against the side of the Kracori's head. The Level-2 bolt—not normally lethal to a Kracori—was in this case, delivered point blank and to a softer part of the skull. The star-hot ball of plasma entered the skull cavity and set about boiling the brain, building up pressure from within. Adam didn't have time to cover his face before the alien's head exploded, drenching him in a putrid mass of blood and brain matter. It got in everything, his mouth, his nose, his eyes and even his ears.

Disgusted and sick to his stomach, Adam shoved the corpse away before rising to his knees and spitting out the foul remains. Callie Morrison stood nearby with the MK held loosely at her side. She, too, had been bathed in alien brain, but not to the same degree as Adam. He wanted to thank her for potentially saving his life, but he wasn't sure if his current state was any better.

"How about a little warning next time," he managed to say.

"You're welcome. What the hell was that thing? He was about to kill you, the famous Adam Cain."

"Hey, he wouldn't have been the first. It can happen."

"Funny."

Adam got to his feet, looking first at the dead Kracori and then at Callie. It was hard to tell if she was injured or not through all the blood and gunk covering her from head to toe. Adam wondered how one brain could cover two people so thoroughly.

"So, what is it?"

"It's a Kracori."

"I never heard of them. But damn, they be tough."

"If you only knew—"

Just then another massive explosion rocked the building, seemingly directly above their head.

"Damn, the battle is still going on upstairs," he said as he moved toward the open portal to the room. There were no other guards present; either they were dead or had moved to other parts of the building to take up the fight.

"Mike, what's your status?"

"Hanging in there. But we could use some help. Another couple of squads showed up out front. We've cleared your building but the damn aliens have moved down the street."

"Did you see anyone come out wearing a white suit?"

"White suit? Even if he was, it ain't white no more. But maybe. There was some bigwig they hustled next door. I don't think the neighbor was too happy about that."

"Okay, we're coming up. We'll collect whatever weapons we can find, otherwise, were unarmed."

"Jay went back to the car for more ammo. Aren't you glad now that we were over prepared, as you said?"

"I'll never question your decisions again."

"Bullshit. It's what you do."

Adam and Callie couldn't believe their eyes. What had once been an exquisite neighborhood of palatial estates now looked like a smoldering warzone. At least four of the homes—including Qallen's—had suffered some degree of damage, with the main estate a crumbling mass of stone, metal and burning wood. Bodies lay everywhere, and cars were blown to bits with fires raging all around.

Adam and Callie could barely make it out of the ruins and onto the smoke-filled driveway. An RPG lit off on the grounds to the east before slamming into the front façade of the neighboring house. Adam didn't see any enemy, but Jay and Mike must have. Either that or they were just blowing off steam as the battle wound down.

"We're in the clear," Adam announced through the comm.

"I see you," said General Oakes. "Heading your way. The boys are still doing target practice next door. Okay guys, knock it off. I think they got the message."

The burly figure of Todd Oakes appeared out of the cloud of black smoke. He had a pair of M88s hooked around his shoulders and another one cradled in his arms.

"Anyone get hurt?" Adam asked as the officer approached.

"You mean other than the two of you? Nothing serious, just a few cuts and bruises."

Callie was still wiping away Kracori blood from her face. Chunks of pink flesh clung desperately to her torn blouse. Oakes surveyed her. "Are you all right," he asked.

She winched as she felt the back of her head. "I'll be okay. I had a door land on me."

Oakes turned his attention to Adam and frowned.

"I'm okay, too," Adam said. "It's Kracori blood."

"Kracori?" Todd Oakes was old enough to have fought in the battle of the Dysion Void thirty years ago. He was a young ensign at the time but that wasn't something one forgot, no matter how old you got. "That's right; I heard you mention the name before I got distracted with the battle. You met a live Kracori?"

"A formerly-live Kracori," Adam smirked, "Thanks to Callie. She saved my life."

"I was getting bored watching the two of you fight."

Adam turned back to Oakes. "But the biggest surprise of the day is that the Clan of the Hood is made up of Kracori."

Oakes shook his head. "I thought we nuked their planet. Aren't they extinct?"

"We did, but some survived. I knew that even before running into this bastard. But it seems some of them have moved off planet and are now mucking things up across the galaxy."

Oakes had trouble accepting the premise. "The Clan *are* the Kracori? All of the Clan?"

"That I don't know, but it would explain why they wear hoods. Someone is bound to recognize them, and that would lead them right back to their homeworld of Elision."

"That's going to take a little getting used to," said the general. "Not sure what all this means for the galaxy."

"Yeah, I'm not sure either. Just one more mystery to ponder."

Adam turned toward the husk of a building that had once been the headquarters for a major counterfeiting operation. "Damn, you guys sure did make a mess. I'll be damned if I'm going to help clean it up."

Just then, Mike ran up, still cradling a loaded RPG.

"Run out of things to blow up?" Callie asked Mike.

Adam noticed how her eyes lit up when Mike smiled at her. Although Callie and Adam had been a pair for the first couple of weeks of the journey to Lo'roan, Adam had noticed the chemistry building between Mike and her. He'd also noticed a cooling of the passion between he and Callie; now he understood why.

"Where's Jay?" Oakes asked.

"He went into the building," Mike said. "He wanted to see the counterfeiting room. Is it still intact?"

Adam nodded. "The last time we checked it was."

"Then let's go," Mike said with a sinister grin.

"The chips are counterfeit," General Oakes pointed out.

"Yeah, but who will know, right? And we do need more operating capital."

He had a point.

It was perilous going back into the basement. Part of the ceiling had collapsed in the printing room making a mess of the operation. Jay was there, shoveling thin, plastic chips into a box he'd found.

"Be careful trying to pass those," Oakes said to the young man. "If you're caught they may arrest you."

"Hey, a thousand here, a thousand there. Even if they find out they're fake, I can plead ignorance, say I got them from someone else."

"That shouldn't be hard for you—pleading ignorance," Mike said with a grin.

Then Jay asked, "What are these?"

The team gathered around one of the printing presses that wasn't covered in debris. Jay was pulling a thin metal sheet off the drum.

"It looks like a printing plate," Callie said. She moved to the next machine and removed the one from there. "This one is for a thousand unit denomination."

There were five machines in the room but they could only get to the drums on two of them.

"What are you going to do with the plates?" Adam asked Jay. "You're not thinking about going into the counterfeiting business, are you? Besides, you know it's all about the chips they're printed on, with all the electronic gizmos in them, that matters most."

"Yeah, but these things may be worth money to someone. And we can't leave them here. The bad guys will just put them on other machines."

Adam shrugged. "Whatever. Keep them if you want. But now it's time to get out of here. Either the bad guys are going to bring in reinforcements or the Security Force is going to show up, and I'm pretty sure I may have violated a tenet or two of their restrictions. The cops we talked to were on the take, but there's another group that wanted these guys gone. With luck, they'll still pay the fee; we earned it. Not only did we find out who the counterfeiters are, but we also shut down the operation. This should make Tidus happy. But now, we have bigger fish to fry, and it only took us a day to wrap up this one. I say mission accomplished. Time to head into the Devil's Gate."

Once back aboard the *Arieel*, Adam contacted the Durin Security Force headquarters and spoke again to the original supervisor. He told him about the two officers in the room with Qallen and how embarrassing it would be for that information to get out. Basically, Adam blackmailed the officer into signing off on the bounty and passing the paperwork up the chain. When Adam broke the link, he was feeling pretty good about himself even as the officer was about to explode. But there was nothing he could do at that point. He was a dirty cop, and Adam wasn't afraid to expose him. He had to cooperate.

10

After a relaxing night on Lo'roan, where everyone nursed their wounds—with Mike tenderly caring for Callie—the next day was spent transferring weapons and equipment to the *Arieel* from the *Farragut*. Todd Oakes had come prepared for just about any contingency, as evidenced by the overabundance of RPGs in the inventory. His preparedness saved Adam and Callie's life. And now having an arsenal crammed into the *Arieel*'s hold, Adam felt more confident with the upcoming bank job. One could never have too much firepower.

By four that afternoon, the *Arieel* lifted from the surface of Lo'roan, leaving the *Farragut* in a secure lot at the spaceport. They would pick it up on the way out of the area.

Their destination was the planet Josilin-Bor, which was one of the nine civilized worlds beyond the Gate. It was only six light-years from Lo'roan and involved transiting the famous passage.

Adam's best comparison to the Devil's Gate was Earth's Suez Canal. Since gravity-drive ships required space free of rogue gravity sources, the cluster of blackholes in the area created a deadly and constantly changing landscape for travelers. Ironically, the safest region was a narrow passageway between the two largest singularities, where their tug-of-war for influence kept the area relatively clear of gravity sources. Even so, the passage was constantly monitored and the path modified to account for ever-changing conditions. An organization of professional transit pilots guided ships through the Gate, sometimes as few as a single ship at a time, as the forces of gravity dictated.

As the *Arieel* waited in a sea of other starships for her turn to make the run, Adam stood by the cockpit viewport, reflecting on how smart the Klin were to choose the Devil's Gate as the location for their largest colony. It was isolated, and entry could be screened and controlled. That was why the *Farragut* wasn't allowed through. There was an unspoken prohibition on warships—from either side—making the transit. That didn't mean spies didn't come and go, including whole military units that set up shop on either side of the Gate, again from both sides. The Klin maintained monitoring stations, as did the Allies.

Most of the major powers in the galaxy—what there were left of them—had at least a token covert presence in the region since they seldom shared information with each other. The Juireans didn't share with the Humans and vice versa, so each had their own operations running. Even so, most governments used surrogates to do the actual spying for them. Humans and Juireans would stand out on all the worlds within the Gate just as a Klin would attract attention walking in the Telegraph Hill neighborhood of San Francisco.

In spite of his melancholy mood, Adam was still entranced by the glowing spectacle of the Devil's Gate. He'd seen a lot of wondrous phenomena throughout the galaxy, but this had to be one of the most incredible. All around were impossibly large clouds of stellar gas, illuminated with every color of the rainbow, twisted into swirling ribbons and energized by the effects of space-distorting gravity. Most of the black-holes had jets of supercharged gas escaping from their poles forming beacons of light that marked their location. Even without the jets, the holes could be detected, as gas spiraled into the maelstroms before disappearing from view at the event horizon. Although Adam was too far away to see any of the actual black holes, he knew they were there, being dwarfed by the overwhelming size of the gas clouds streaming into them.

From his vantage point, Adam saw multiple stellar clouds filling the vast expanse of space, although he could not comprehend their size. Each cloud covered a light-year or two, and with some up to four LYs in width. He tried to imagine a structure so large that it could fill the gap between the Sun and Alpha Centauri, a distance of four light-years. It was incomprehensible, so Adam didn't even try. Instead, he simply took in the wonder and accepted it for what it was: Just another day in the marvelous and mysterious Milky Way Galaxy.

Too bad such a beautiful place had to be populated with such filthy, degenerate creatures, such as Klin, Juireans, Kracori … and yes, Humans.

The Kracori Ludiff, Benavee Plin, stepped from the transport and was instantly swarmed over by the fidgety Inerian crime boss Qallen Laznick. It had been three days since the attack on the printing plant and the alien had acquired another wardrobe of all white. Since the building had been his home, all his clothing was destroyed, yet he wasted no time replacing it, at least part of it.

"Welcome, my Ludiff," said the offensive creature,

using Benavee's formal title, although it wasn't an official moniker. There hadn't been an *official* Ludiff of the Kracori in almost thirty standard years. "I know this visit was scheduled in advance; however, I know it must sadden you to know that a brother of the Clan died in the melee. There are so few of you that any loss is a tragedy."

"There are more of us than you realize," Benavee stated firmly. The statement wasn't entirely true, but he didn't want the alien to get the impression that the Clan's small numbers were a sign of weakness. "Take me to the room, I wish to survey the damage."

"Of course."

Qallen, and a small entourage of Durin officials, accompanied Benavee as he entered the ruins of the once magnificent residence, being careful of the still fragile walls and remnants of the shattered roof. The surrounding neighborhood was also in shambles, and only on this day had others began to return to assess the damage to their homes.

"The Humans did all this?" Benavee asked. He'd seen the report, but now he questioned it.

"Yes, my Ludiff. There were two inside and three outside."

"I saw the report; you invited two of them into the building, even paraded them through the plant. Why would you do such a foolish act?"

Qallen turned another shade lighter, almost to the

point where his skin matched the pure white of his clothing. "It was a mistake, I now realize. But the one known as *The Human* was on Lo'roan. He is a recovery agent of some notoriety. I admit to my curiosity. Even so, it was the three outside who caused most of the damage. They came prepared with explosives and ballistic weapons for which our flash weapons were no match."

"There was a *team* of Humans?"

"Apparently," Qallen answered. "We were unaware of the three following."

"Casualties?"

"We lost one hundred nine."

"And the Humans?"

"My Ludiff?"

"How many did the Humans lose?"

"None. I thought that was obvious."

Benavee stopped to stare at the pale-skinned alien. "Only five Humans inflicted all this damage and they did not suffer any losses of their own? Are your people that incompetent? When the Clan agreed to sponsor your operation we were led to believe you were a major force on Lo'roan. You had sources in the government and beings on the streets. You told us you had an army." He looked once again at the still smoldering ruins. "And yet only five Humans did all this to your home and to your so-called *army*."

"Forgive me, my Ludiff, but they *are* Humans. You must know of the stories."

Benavee did, better than most.

Even though he was young at the time of the *Harrowing*, he lived through the aftermath and knew who was directly responsible: It was the Humans. Although the Juireans had participated in what others called the Battle of the Dysion Void, the green-skinned aliens chose to pursue the fleeing Klin Colony Ships instead of the Kracori. It was the Human fleet that descended upon Benavee's homeworld of Elision and unleashed radioactive purgatory upon the land. He had been one of the lucky ones, residing in a faraway rural community at the time and away from the major cities. The aliens sent their missiles to where most of the population lived, leaving the rest of the race to suffer through the aftermath: the radiation sickness and agonizing death; the starvation; the disease and the degradation as the *Legend* of the Kracori came to a tragic end—at least for the time being.

Members of the same race that committed the *Harrowing* had done this to Qallen's home, even as they once did far worse to Benavee's. Yes, he'd heard the stories; he had *lived* them.

The Ludiff cast off his anger to concentrate on the here and now. The counterfeit operation in Lo'roan was one of the Clan's most lucrative endeavors, Of the eighty-eight million in total that was acquired last year, this single plant contributed over thirty million, even after splitting with the locals. Its loss would be a major setback, affecting the timetable by a significant amount. Benavee was not a patient Kracori, so the delay only infuriated him more.

As they climbed through the rubble and then down a smokey and foul-smelling stairway, Qallen sensed the Ludiff's mood and offered a bit of good news.

"As best as we can determine, about half the chip masters survived, so we can resume operation as soon as the presses are replaced, along with the plates."

Benavee was distracted by the disappointing scene he saw at the base of the stairs. All five machines were damaged to some degree, with three completely buried in debris from the collapsed ceiling. The printing masters were strewn across the floor, having been stomped on by the first natives surveying the damage. Did they realize how valuable the masters were? Their manufacture—which was another major operation of the Clan—cost a full third of the face value of a counterfeit chip. Add to that the loss from direct confiscation, and that was why out of every thousand-unit chip, the Clan only realized a profit of thirty percent. Yes, the public numbers were impressive, speaking of the production of tens of millions of artificial energy credits. But in the end, it took that much to justify the cost.

And here aliens were crushing the chips with the soles of their shoes.

And then something Qallen said resurfaced in Benavee's consciousness.

"You mentioned the plates?"

"Yes, three remain in the buried presses, but two are missing."

"Missing ... as in stolen?"

Qallen was taken aback. "Not by my people, I assure you! I have been here almost every hour since the attack, me and my supervisors. In addition, Security Force personal—all under my influence—have been guarding the premises. I wanted to assure that none of the finished inventory was taken. As best as we can determine there are about nine million in printed credits still in the room. We will have a more accurate count once we begin clearing the debris. I assure you, my Ludiff, I will have ample security to protect against theft."

Benavee moved to the closest press and began digging through the broken concrete from the upper floors. He knew where to look, and after a minute of searching he came upon the drum. The printing plate was still attached to the press, but it was badly damaged, useless. He looked at what he could see of the other machines. The plates would not have survived.

Then he looked over at the two undamaged

presses, which was a misnomer; all had suffered some degree of damage, just some more than others. The shiny drums were clearly visible with the plates gone.

Qallen and the Kracori moved to one of the presses. Benavee pointed. "You can see, the drum is undamaged. I must assume so was the plate. Who took them, and why?"

It was not a rhetorical question; Benavee demanded an answer.

"I cannot speak for sure, but it was reported that the Humans reentered the building after the battle. Perhaps they took them."

"Why?"

"Unknown, but perhaps to sell. We both know how rare and expensive they are."

"Yes I do. I also know that without the masters to accompany them, it is virtually impossible to make counterfeit energy credits. Without them, the plates would not have much value."

"The two of us know as much, my Ludiff, but would others? And if they only printed a few on standard chips, and then passed them through smaller transactions on more primitive planets, their detection would be more difficult."

"Where are the Humans now?" Benavee growled.

"They took one of their two vessels to the Gate."

Benavee stared at the nervous alien, pleased to see that his stark white garment was already marked with soot and other stains. "They did not return to their worlds?"

"No, my Ludiff," Qallen reported. Then quickly: "If you wish, I will place more inquiries. They may not have made the passage as of yet."

"Yes, track them. And even if they make it through, track them still. I want those plates. There are no replacements at the moment, and to have new ones made will take half a standard year. I cannot afford to have this operation dormant for so long."

"As you wish, my Ludiff. Should I send units in pursuit of the Humans?"

"No, track them only. I will take my Clan mates and go personally. We have contacts beyond the Devil's Gate. Besides, I would be anxious to retrieve the plates myself, while encountering these mythical beings for my own. And I assure you, Qallen, unlike you, I will not invite the Humans in for refreshments and conversation. I will not underestimate these evil beings, not as you did."

11

The transit through the Devil's Gate was a unique experience for Adam and the others. It involved being tethered to four other ships and then towed through the opening as if the vessels were part of a cargo string being hauled by a muleship. The lead vessel, a monster of a ship, used a single gravity-well to tow the string, keeping the gravity influences to a minimum. The transit only took ninety minutes but it involved a number of elaborate course changes made by the pilot ship following an intricate maze of accommodating curvatures in space.

Adam had to wait for nineteen hours before the *Arieel* was scheduled for the passage, during which time the team inventoried their weapons while doing their best to store things away in the limited space aboard the starship. The *Arieel* was not built for five passengers.

It only had two small staterooms. For most of the journey to Lo'roan, that wasn't a problem since they also had access to the *Farragut*. But now the sleeping arrangements became more nuanced.

Adam and Callie found time to hash out their relationship issues, with her admitting she now had a thing for Mike Hannon, and the feeling was mutual. That meant the lovers were given one of the staterooms aboard the *Arieel*, while the other three males hot-racked the remaining bed. That was fine, that left each of them with eight hours to have the room to themselves, leaving the others to hang out in the small common room or the cockpit.

The main problem was the cargo hold. It wasn't very big and it was now packed with weapons, ammo and other sundry equipment General Oakes had brought along for the bank job. He had no idea what they would be going up against at the time he gathered the inventory, so he brought just about anything he could get his hands on. That was fine for this stage of the operation, but Adam was wondering where would they put all the energy credits they were hoping to appropriate?

Knowing the dimensions of the security crates, Adam began measuring every square foot of the *Arieel*, drawing out plans for where to stow the hundred containers they were expecting. They would be everywhere, in the staterooms, the common room and even the spine corridor. Once they got back to the *Farragut*, they'd have no problem. The destroyer had plenty of room since it was built for a crew of twenty-five.

Adam and the others couldn't help but speculate on what they would encounter during the heist. But since none of them knew for sure, it was a fruitless and frustrating endeavor. Still, their minds wouldn't rest, leaving all five Humans chomping at the bit to get the mission started.

All nine planets beyond the Gate were located fairly close to each other and all clustered within a sphere eight light-years in diameter. Josilin-Bor was the closest to the Gate and was where the team was to meet with their undercover source to acquire the schematics to the bank building, along with more details about the security system and defensive forces protecting the site.

It had already been discussed with the General's other sources that the bank was lightly guarded. It was a Klin facility in a Klin-dominated neighborhood, and unlike Humans—as well as just about any other race—they didn't steal from themselves, only others.

The bank was on the planet Arancus, where most of the Klin in the Colony lived. Of the two and a half million Klin fighters stranded in the Milky Way at the end of their failed invasion, over nine hundred thousand came to the planets of the Devil's Gate, with an estimated six hundred thousand on Arancus. They congregated in three main cities, where they did their best to assimilate into the native population in order to muddle the target should the Allies decided to take them out. By living within the native population, it would make a full-scale attack less likely.

But the natives and the Klin didn't mesh well, even as the Klin set about making themselves valuable to the inhabitants of the Devil's Gate. The natives prospered with the technology and new products they could produce and sell, but that didn't make them like the Klin any better. They were still the silver-skinned bastards who had been mucking up the galaxy for over four thousand years, whether it be from the native Klin or those who came over recently from the Newfound Galaxy.

And then the Klin also made it hard for the natives to accept them. They treated other aliens as, well, aliens, giving them no respect and degrading them every chance they got, whether it was intentional or not. The Klin had an attitude of superiority that was ingrained in their personality. They couldn't help but be assholes.

What this produced was a progressive separation of the populations between the Klin and the Natives. As the years went by, and the Allies proved their reluctance to upset the applecart, the Klin felt more comfortable forming their own communities. One such enclave was called Sylox, a mountain retreat where over a hundred thousand Klin lived. It was the closest to the bank. All this information was available to General Oakes from the intelligence gathered by native spies on the payroll of the Allies. The Klin were under constant surveillance, with the Allies watching for any indication that the silver-skinned bastards were planning provocative actions. So far, they hadn't. But these were the Klin. It was just a matter of time before they'd try something again, and the Allies had four thousand years of Klin history as proof.

But Josilin-Bor wasn't Arancus. It had a much smaller Klin population, mainly consisting of their own intelligence service agents who monitored the Gate. Even so, Adam and the others felt uncomfortable as they drove a rented transport to meet the confidential source. Klin were openly walking the streets, comfortable with Josilin-Bor's six-tenths gravity as compared to Earth's. Klin were famously thin-boned and weak-muscled, at least the Milky Way Klin were. That was why they needed surrogate races to do their fighting for them. But this new breed that had flooded through a trans-dimensional portal from the Newfound Galaxy were a hardier breed, tougher and more resilient—and much better fighters. They were also less nuanced and conniving as their Milky Way brothers and sisters. If they didn't like you they would let you know to your face rather than maneuver behind your back to stab you. In that way, Adam respected the New

Klin more, at least as one respected the danger presented by a spitting cobra. He still wanted to kill every last one of them he saw. And so far, he'd seen about a dozen on the streets of this nameless city on Josilin-Bor.

12

The confidential source was located in an industrial section of the town in a warehouse with half a dozen security cameras blatantly attached to the walls outside. It wasn't subtle, letting Adam know that the source was sending a message to anyone even thinking about robbing him: You will be watched. And who knew what other security measures he had for protection. Adam figured he wouldn't have gone through so much trouble unless it was necessary.

The General took the lead since he was the only one in the group who had spoken with the native. Todd Oakes stood at a solid metal door and waited patiently for his identity to be verified. A voice came through a hidden speaker.

"Why have you brought so many of your kind?"

The sound was tinny, either from the speaker or the alien.

"They are my team. You should have expected as much, considering the target."

"Foolishness, but I will not judge. You came upon me unexpectedly. But enter."

The door sprung open and the five Humans moved inside.

Unlike the grubby neighborhood the warehouse was in, the interior of the building was modern and clean, made up of a short foyer separated from a large work area by double half walls with strong metal columns rising to an open-beam ceiling fifty feet above.

The native was an electronics expert, one of the specialists hired to wire the Klin bank with sophisticated alarms and locks. There were several teams working on the building at the time, so no single individual knew the system completely. That was a problem, but the alien assured the general that he had a source of his own who could fill in most of the blanks.

The native was of an alien species Adam had seen before. He was a short, round, purple-skinned creature with four arms, two upper dominate appendages and two short ones called min-arms. These were used primarily for feeding the lower stomach, which the alien could do even while talking. The mouth and lungs were on two different systems. In a way, it made sense. One could talk and eat at the same time and it wasn't considered rude.

"This is Unonen/Linn," General Oakes said to the team. "He has been in our service since the Klin first arrived. As you know, the Klin have been in the Devil's Gate for about five years, arriving two years before the end of the invasion. They didn't conquer the worlds here, but rather used the area as a discrete staging area for some of their activities here, and in the Kidis Frontier. Things changed after the invasion failed and they brought most of their survivors here. How have you been, Unonen?"

The purple alien eyed the team with undisguised suspicion and concern. Although the Klin practiced a live-and-let live existence within the Devil's Gate, they still didn't tolerate spies and turncoats.

As Adam eyed the creature, he had a tremendous moment of déjà vu thinking of the other Lip'polin he'd known before—the underhanded, conniving Lion/El from Adam's adopted homeworld of Navarus. Seeing the purple-skinned creature sent memories cascading through Adam's cloned brain. They weren't bad memories; neither were they especially good. They were just memories of a long and eventful life—right up until the point where Adam died—and then was cloned. That would mess up anyone's sense of perspective.

"I am well, but unprepared."

"You knew we were coming," Oakes said.

"After a delay, you said."

Todd shrugged. "Well, we weren't delayed as long as we thought. What do you have for us?"

"Twenty-five thousand energy credits first."

Todd smirked. "Yeah, sure. Jay…"

Jay Williford pulled the credits from a canvas satchel he had hooked over his shoulder. Adam smirked. Originally, the team had twenty-five thousand credits set aside for this transaction. But after Jay raided the counterfeiter's stash, they suddenly had a whole lot more, even if they were counterfeit. But Unonen didn't know they were fake. It may not be the most ethical of transactions, but Adam was much more pragmatic these days, as was everyone in the galaxy. Looking out for number one was the law of the land, and Adam had no problem obeying that particular law, even as he regularly skirted other rules and regulations when the time called for it.

Once paid, the alien became much more relaxed. He went to his computer and pulled up a file. The team gathered around the device.

"I have copied what information I was allowed to have at the time of the installation, and then summarized from memory other aspects. It was many years ago. The bank was built even before the formal occupation as a storage facility for the Klin's other bounty."

"Can you translate that into English—Human

language?" Adam asked. He couldn't read alien, but the computer should have a conversion option. It did, and a moment later the team was scanning the information prior to it being transferred to a scan disk. As it was with most such translations, it was awkwardly phrased, but they could understand it.

"This is mainly about the security lines," Callie said. "It's not much use without a schematic of the building as a whole."

"Precisely," said the alien. "That is why I need more time. I have a source on Arancus with the schematics. Now that you are here, I will contact him. You must leave now and return tomorrow."

"You can't link with him now?" Jay Williford asked.

"There are protocols. He is in the employ of the Klin. Later. Return tomorrow. Then I will give you the information."

"We'll take this data now," Todd said referring to the information on the screen. The alien had twenty-five thousand credits—albeit counterfeit credits—and the general didn't want to leave without getting something for his money.

Unonen swept a chip over the scan port and then handed it to the general. "Return in the morning for the rest. Now go and avoid contact with the Klin. Humans are not welcome in Devil's Gate, although there are some. But they mainly remain in their Diplomatic missions and rarely wander the streets."

"What's it like on Arancus?" Mike asked, referring to the planet where the bank was located.

"Even more so than here. Humans are not restricted; that would provoke the Allies too much. Even so, the Klin appear to have an innate fear of anything Human. It is quite irrational."

Adam didn't think so. But then again, he knew a lot more about the Klin invasion than anyone in the room, including the general. Maybe someday, he'd explain it to people. That, or he'd put it in a book. He had no doubt it would be a bestseller.

The team left the warehouse, and following the advice of the alien, returned to the *Arieel*.

Callie and Jay huddled over the data regarding the security system to the building. Without context provided by the schematics, it wasn't of much use, but still the two computer experts on the team studied the data, gaining insight into the principle behind it.

Adam studied the navigation charts. The planet Arancus was six and a half light-years from here, or about six hours. The speed limit within the Devil's Gate was more restrictive than in other parts of the galaxy because of the constant eddies and undercurrents created by the surrounding black holes and swirling gas clouds. Even though diaphanous, the clouds still had considerable mass which warped space in unpredictable ways. Normally, six-point-five light-years could be traversed in a couple of hours. But not here. Here it would take six hours.

More than anyone else on the team, Adam was more aware of the passage of time. He hadn't told Tidus about the side mission, so the longer he stayed away from Tel'oran, the more suspicious he'd become. And he could track the *Arieel* if he wanted. If he became curious, he could locate the ship in the Devil's Gate and wonder why he made the trip. Sightseeing? The place was a tourist trap thanks to the unique topography of space in the region. But Adam wasn't much of a tourist, not after all the years he'd spent in space.

Adam didn't dwell much on the excuse, hoping he wouldn't need it. Tomorrow, they'd get the schematics, then a six-hour flight to Arancus. The planning of the actual attack was already in the works, using the combined experience of the team of Humans. It wasn't precise, but Adam approached it as he would any siege, as he did in the SEALs planning a rescue mission. But this mission was to rescue as much of a half a billion in energy credits that they could liberate from its Klin prison. The parts of the operation were all the same: A location, a security consideration and protective units. Then there was the exfiltration, leaving the area with the hostage/credits. In principal, the planning was the same. Only the details varied. With the file tomorrow, and an on-site survey of the building, there was no reason to delay action. A quick in and a quick out. Then back to Tel'oran with a fortune in energy credits. And with no one coming after them for stealing the money. Adam liked the sound of that. A lot.

13

"They did not stay long," Ludiff Benavee Plin commented.

"Less than twenty minutes," said the spy.

The hooded figure turned his dark shroud to the native. "Did they bring anything with them; did they leave with anything?"

"One was carrying a pouch. He had it when he left, but nothing else, as I could tell."

"And who is in the building?"

"A native technician named Unonen/Linn. His family is well-known here although he has business throughout Devil's Gate."

The spy wasn't a Lip'polin, but rather a shade-variant able to change the color of his skin to match a background. His kind were popular in the secretive trades, able to move nearly invisibly in certain environments. The Clan used them extensively since the Kracori form was unable to move in groups without being noticed.

Benavee nodded and then turned to the three other Clan members with him. They made an ominous spectacle; nearly eight-foot-tall and covered in the grey cloak and grey hood with its blacked-out mesh interior. They wore gloves so even their hands were not exposed. Benavee longed for the time when this disguise could be discarded, when the Kracori could once again show their face in the galaxy and have species tremble and bow whenever they came near. His race had never had the chance to fulfill that promise, a promise made long ago by the evil Klin. The Kracori *Legend* was to stand beside the Klin as leaders of the galaxy, the Kracori *force* to the Klin's *cerebral* management. At the time, the Kracori accepted their role; they cherished the idea of being the superior strength in the galaxy. But even then, they never fully accepted their role as co-leaders. Eventually, their strength and superior Legend would supplant the Klin, leaving only the Kracori to rule.

Unfortunately, that was not to be. And much of the responsibility for the Kracori loss of Legend came from the race of beings he had followed to this rundown warehouse district—the enigmatic Humans.

Benavee grew up hearing the stories and despising the Human race. At this moment, he would just as soon slaughter every last one of them, beginning with these five. But first he needed to recover his printing plates. Undoubtedly, they were within the building.

The spy told them about the building's security features, at least those on the outside. Many were evident, although the Ludiff knew those were only the ones meant to be seen. He didn't fear the occupant. All he had to make sure was that the native did not get away—and with the plates.

And that was why Benavee decided to dispense with subtlety and sent his team in using a sonic battering ram, blasting the door inward and then rushing in with a support team of ten made up of various races, including two Lip'polin natives.

The native occupant was seated at a worktable and was caught by surprise. He tumbled to the floor and began crawling away. With his four arms and two legs he was as fast as most two-legged creatures. Even so, he didn't get far. Soon, he was placed on a stool and surrounded by aliens with guns.

The Ludiff walked up to him, using his superior size and intimidating clothing to send terror into the heart of his prisoner. Benavee said nothing for a full minute, instead the dark abyss of his hood appearing as a true representation of the Gate to Hell.

And then he spoke.

"You had visitors earlier, a group of Humans. I am here to recover my property, property they stole from me. Return it and you shall live. Resist and you will die."

There was no question what Benavee said was the truth.

Unonen tried to speak, but his mouth was so dry that he only squeaked. He tried to moisten his lips but there was no fluid with which to do it.

"Get him water," Benavee commanded.

Once a glass was presented, Unonen was able to speak.

"I know not what you mean. The Humans did not leave any—" And then his yellow eyes grew wide. "Do you refer to the credits? Yes! I have twenty-five thousand credits. I will get them for you. You may take them."

The Lip'polin tried to leave the stool but was restrained by the guards.

"It is not credits we seek. What was it the Humans sold you?"

Unonen squinted and his head bobbed. "Sold ... me? No, I did not purchase from them. They purchased from *me*."

Benavee stepped back, growing impatient with the alien's lies.

"I know that is not the truth. The Humans brought printing plates to you. You bought them. I want them back."

"Please believe me! I know not of what you speak. I

bought nothing from the Humans. They were here to buy information, that is all."

Benavee studied the pleading creature, seeing the fear in his eyes and on his body. Could he be telling the truth?

"They did not sell you the plates?"

"No!"

Benavee turned to a colleague. "They must still have them," he said.

The dark face of the second Clan member turned to Unonen. "What shall we do with this one? I suggest we kill him so he will not warn the Humans that we are tracking them."

Benavee nodded. He knew what his Clan mate was saying: *He* wanted to kill the purple alien. The Kracori had so few chances to kill these days as they were more managers of their expanding criminal enterprise and rarely interacted at the local level. Where they operated there were so few opportunities to experience the cathartic exercise of killing an intelligent being. And since Jessin had first raised the subject, he was entitled to do the honors.

Unonen heard the conversation; the Kracori were not shy about revealing their intentions. A foul smell rose up from the stool as the alien defecated from the fear. "No, do not do this. I will not tell anyone. I promise—" Just then, the native's eyes grew larger and his breathing began fluttering. "I … I will tell you why the Humans were here. They came not to sell but to buy. I have information, information worth millions of credits."

The two Kracori turned to the trembling prisoner. "What are you speaking of?" asked Jessin.

"A bank! A Klin bank on Arancus. The Humans came seeking information about the bank."

"Why?"

"It is my feelings that they wish to steal from the Klin."

Benavee turned to Jessin. "The Humans as thieves? Does that seem strange?"

"They are a savage and disloyal race. Yes, they can steal."

"A half a billion credits," Unonen cried out. "That is what I have heard. There is a half a billion credits in the bank."

This got the attention of the Kracori. For several years while operating under the veil of the Clan, the Kracori had been accumulating credits, millions of them, to be used to purchase ships and weapons of war. After the cleansing of the traditional power structure within the galaxy by the Klin invasion, the Kracori saw an opening to fill the void created by the collapse of both the Juirean Expansion and the Human's Orion-Cygnus Union. But the Kracori were few and without the industrial capacity to rebuild their war fleet. The only option was to buy the war machines from others. And there were plenty of willing sellers, including the proverbial Maris-Kliss and Xan-fi organizations. Especially Xan-fi.

As the second largest manufacturing company in the galaxy, their stock had dropped significantly when it was learned they were in partners with the Milky Way Klin in the development of subcutaneous slave crawlers that could enslave trillions. And they did, until a way was found to override the devices. Then the galaxy turned on the huge weapons manufacturer. Although they were still a viable company, they also had an abundance of inventory which they could not sell. The Kracori had already negotiated with them. All the Clan needed were the credits. The fleet was available—for the right price.

And a half a billion energy credits would go a long way to reaching their goal. And stealing the credit from a Klin bank would be much faster than their current path.

"What is this information you sold them?" Benavee demanded.

"Electronics, alarm systems and schematics of the bank and the systems involved."

"The Humans have this information now?" Benavee could envision a race to the bank.

"No, not all of it. They are to return tomorrow for the rest."

"Explain."

"I gave them part, but only moments ago did I get the schematics. Without the plans, the information I gave the Humans earlier is virtually useless. For my life, I will give all the information to you." Unonen looked anxiously from dark abyss of the face to dark abyss. There were no emotions to read so the alien knew not if his bargain was being considered.

"Your life for the information," said Benavee. He did not elaborate, his mind already made up as to the final outcome. "Very well, give us the information."

"Yes! Yes!"

Unonen turned to his computer and began to run transfer chips over the port.

"The alarm system, and now the schematics. Also, location of the bank and other observations I have just received from my on-site source. This is all you will need. Take it, take it all. It is yours."

Benavee took the data chips and placed them in a pouch within his cloak. He turned away.

"Then it is done?" Unonen asked. "Our bargain is complete? I will be spared?"

"The bargain is complete," Benavee said as he walked toward the open portal where the door once stood. "However, you cannot be spared. You must not live to alert the Humans or anyone else of the bank and the treasures it holds. "Jessin, you spoke first. You shall take his *Legend*, what there is of it."

The Ludiff's remarks had barely been absorbed by

the alien's feeble brain when Jessin produced a two-foot-long sword from under his cloak. The metal blade had a hair-thin wire infused along the edge that heated to two thousand degrees instantly. When the Kracori passed the sword through the middle torso of the four-armed creature, it met no resistance of flesh or bone. Instead, it simply severed the Lip'polin in half.

The cut was so clean and spontaneous that the two halves rested perfectly together. Unonen's body would remain like this, with his head slumped forward appearing asleep, until someone came along to disturb it.

14

It was Adam and his four Human friends the next morning who disturbed the body.

It was Day-3 on Josilin-Bor when the team returned to Unonen's warehouse. Finding the outer security door blown open, they drew their Human ballistic weapons and approached with caution.

Adam was the first through the door, with Callie and Mike covering him. Then Mike slipped in past him, followed by Callie. By the time Jay and the general entered, Adam had already given the all clear. What happened here had happen hours ago, as evidenced by the grey paleness of the alien's once-purple skin.

Adam saw the thin red line from what was miss-named a laser sword. There was no blood, as the high temperature of the cutting wire cauterized the flesh as it passed through. But the trauma was undeniable. Unonen had died instantly.

The team didn't need to wonder why he was killed. The native was a trader of secrets, and the secrets he was going to sell to the Humans that morning was worth a lot of energy credits, much more than a single life was worth. And whoever did this not only knew of the bank, but they now had the information Adam was after. How did Adam know this? The alien was dead, and dead aliens told no tales.

"So, that's it?" Mike said. "We can't do shit without the schematics. Maybe the other guys don't have them either."

"I think they do?" Adam said. "Unonen was going to get them yesterday. He was killed sometime last night."

"So we're fucked." Callie said. "Not only do we not have the schematics, but now there's someone else who knows about the bank. Who could that be?"

"Hell if I know."

"There could be a way to find out," Jay said. He was hovering near Unonen's worktable, looking at the monitors and his computer. The others went over to him.

"An electronics wizard lived here, and he had the outside of his warehouse wired with a half a dozen cameras. And those were just the ones he wanted people to see," Jay said. "You can bet he also had other cameras and sensors around. And the people who killed him had to crash his door to get in. Maybe he had some internal cameras going at the same time."

"So what good is that going to do us?" Mike asked. "Unless we track them down and steal our information back. Information we already paid for, by the way."

"With counterfeit credits," Oakes reminded him.

"I'll get into the computer, see what I can find," Jay said. "We might get lucky."

Adam was amazed watching the young man work his magic on the keyboard. Although the keys were in alien, Jay was able to access a program that changed the letters and symbols to English. Adam didn't even know the feature was available. It would have saved him a lot of aggravation in the past if he had.

Soon, Jay was dancing on the keys, scanning files until he came upon what he was looking for. It was a massive folder of recordings, both from outside the warehouse and inside; in fact, the last file showed the five Humans at the computer terminal watching a video of themselves watching the video. Callie looked in the direction of the camera and waved. Then she flipped them off.

"Great job, son," Adam said, resting a hand on the young man's shoulder. It seemed odd that Adam would refer to Jay as 'son' since Adam looked younger than Jay. "Play it back. And is there sound?"

"Yeah, I got audio, too. Here we go. Timestamp about Night-7."

The recording showed the outer door being blown in by something other than an explosion. Probably a sonic blast, as best Adam could determine. And then in came a horde of people, with four prominent figures in cloaks and hoods. The Kracori.

"What the hell?" Adam said. "They tracked us from Lo'roan. Why?"

Jay turned up the sound and a confusing conversation blared from hidden speakers in the room. At the mention of the printing plates, Adam gazed down at Jay, as did all the others. He didn't look up.

"How was I to know they'd come looking for them."

"They're kind of a big deal in the counterfeiting business," Callie said.

"Hey, you took the plates off the second machine."

Callie just pursed her lips in her defense. "You started it."

It was shortly after that when the scene turned deadly ominous as Unonen/Linn began negotiating for his life—by giving the Clan the information about the Klin bank.

"Goddammit!" General Oakes yelled. "He gave them everything, even the schematics." He looked at his watch. "They also have a nine-hour head start on us."

"That's assuming they're going for the bank," Jay said.

"Oh, they're going for it. The fact that this poor sap is sitting here with his body sliced in two confirms that."

"Then we're screwed," Mike said. "Without the schematics, we have nothing."

"We can try to find the Clan and take them from them," Jay offered.

Adam snorted. "There weren't only four Kracori, but also ten others. The Clan probably have a small army they can call upon in the Devil's Gate. And trust me when I say this, even if they didn't have an army, we don't want to go one-on-one with the Kracori, even as a bunch of badass Humans."

There was a moment of silence while each team member fought for a solution. Finally, Mike said, "Then I guess we head home. We still have a few million counterfeit credits. We might be able to pass them somewhere, at least enough to buy fuel pods to get us back to our homes."

Adam then leaned in closer to the screen. "Jay, run the recording back a little more. Unonen had the schematics to give to the Kracori. That means he made contact with his source on Arancus."

Jay did as he was told, and sure enough, there was a recording of the conversation the alien had with someone on a link and the downloading of data to Unonen's computer.

"Can you find that file?" Adam asked Jay.

"I've already tried. All files received last night have been erased. Unonen did it to assure the Kracori that only they had the information."

"But Unonen's source still has the information. Can you find the link code?"

"You're going to call him?" Callie asked.

"It can't hurt," Adam replied.

"Yep, I got it," Jay said a few seconds later.

"Okay, you guys clear out. I don't want to intimidate this alien with the sight of five Humans staring at him."

"And so you, the alien with an attitude, will be less threatening," Mike said with a shake of his head. "Yeah, right."

"Just stand back and let me show you how it's done."

Jay dialed the link code and it went through almost immediately. The creature on the other side saw the number as that of his friend and was anxious to speak with him again. But when his imaged resolved and he got a look at who was looking back at him, he fainted.

"What the hell!" Adam yelled.

Jay and General Oakes could see the image of the alien, as well, and they echoed Adam's words a split second later.

"It can't be," said Oakes. "All those purple bastards look alike. It can't be him."

"He fainted when he saw Adam," Jay pointed out. "It's him. It's Lion/El."

"Who the hell is Lion/El?" Callie asked.

Adam pulled up a chair and sat down, waiting for the alien to come to. This could get awkward.

"Lion/El was my real estate agent on Navarus," Adam explained. "He also became president of the planet. Jay and Todd knew him, too, from the old days."

"The consummate hustler," Oakes said. "He had his fingers in every shady deal done on the planet."

"What's he doing in the Devil's Gate?" Jay asked.

Adam snorted. "We're on his species' native world. Maybe after the Klin invaded Navarus he came home, and then worked his way to Arancus. Even so, what are the odds?"

"Is he still alive?" Callie asked.

The camera had a facial tracking feature on the other end and was now focused on the sleeping alien on the floor. His lower lip trembled and his eye lids fluttered. He was alive.

"Lion/El!" Adam yelled through the link. "Lion/El … wake up!"

It took another thirty seconds until the yellow eyes opened and the mouth closed, even as a stream of spittle drained down his pointed chin.

"Get up," Adam commanded. "What the hell is wrong with you?"

The rotund, purple alien with four arms staggered to his feet and then poured himself back into a chair. By then, the other Humans were on the screen. Lion/El eked out a thin grin.

"Greetings, Cain-mis. And General Oakes-mis and even Jay Williford. I do not recognize the other Humans." He looked down at his computer. "It says the link is coming from Josilin-Bor. Are you on the planet?"

"You know we are," Adam said.

Having recovered from the shock of seeing Adam again, the alien was quickly regaining his composure and putting on his game face. As Todd said, Lion/El was the consummate hustler. He often didn't lose his cool like this.

"Why did you faint when you saw me?" Adam asked. "We didn't part on bad terms."

"No, we did not." Then he grinned. "I heard of your transformation, Cain-mis. I must say, it *was* a shock to see it in person. Perhaps that was a contributing factor. It is a miracle, your rising from the dead. And after all that happened on Navarus, I am never sure of your attitude toward me. You must understand. Why are you linking with me now?"

"We didn't know we were calling *you*," Adam said. "What are you doing on Arancus?"

"An interesting story. As you know, the Klin came to Navarus after you and the mutants disappeared. They stayed for three years, during which time I served as their liaison with the population of the planet. I impressed them enough that when they moved to the Devil's Gate they took me with them. I am a coordinator of sorts, seeing that the Klin themselves are not welcome in other parts of the galaxy. I serve a purpose and they provide for me."

"What do you know about the Klin bank?" Mike Hannon asked as he was growing tired of beating around the bush.

"The Klin bank? I am sure I know not of which you speak."

"Bullshit," Mike said. "You were working with Unonen/Linn, providing intelligence about the bank."

Lion/El scanned the determined faces of the Humans. Although he was light-years away, his fear of them was evident even on the link. "Yes, I know of this bank, and I was providing information for my friend Unonen. How does this involve you?"

"I was his client," General Oakes said. "You didn't know he was working with Humans?"

Lion/El bobbed his head, which most of the time in alien meant no. "All I knew was it was a party from outside the Gate. He never mentioned it was with Humans. If he had, I would have remembered. Where is he, I do not see him in his work area."

Adam tapped Jay on the shoulder and pointed at the still upright corpse of Unonen/Linn. Jay found the camera with that angle and switched sources.

"Is he conscious?"

Adam stepped into the scene. "Nah, not hardly." Then he shoved on the alien's shoulder. The upper half toppled off the lower half.

"*By the Swams of Gorlin!* What happened to him?"

"The Clan of the Hood happened to him, that's what," Adam announced. "They came in here last night and Unonen gave him all the information that was meant for us, information we already paid for. He got the schematics from you, didn't he? We want them. Send them over now."

Lion/El was feeling groggy, looking as if he was about to pass out again. Adam grimaced. Maybe such a graphic display wasn't a good idea. He just wanted Lion/El to understand how serious the situation was.

"The Clan, they did this?"

"They did, and now they're going after the bank. We have to get there before they do."

Lion/El again scanned the eyes of the Humans. "I thought it foolish when I first heard that someone was planning to assault the Klin bank. Knowing now that it was Humans planning the affair, it has signaled concern. What if the Klin trace your activities back to me?"

"It's not the Klin you need to worry about, it's the Clan."

"Why? Do they know of me?"

"They know Unonen got the information from someone else, and they have the call logs from last night," Adam said, stretching the truth some. He wanted what Lion/El had and a scared alien was a compliant alien.

"Why would they wish to harm me? As you said, they already have the schematics."

"It would be to keep you from giving them to anyone else. But don't worry, Lion/El. We'll protect you."

"From the Clan? From the Klin? I think not."

"Then give us the schematics, and they'll have no reason to hurt you," Oakes said.

Lion/El furrowed his purple brow. "The Clan is going to rob the bank?" he asked.

"We think that's their plan," Oakes confirmed.

"And you wish to rob the bank as well?"

"That's also our plan."

"So, either way, someone is going to rob the bank."

"That's right," Adam said. "We want it to be us and not them."

"Let me summarize my thoughts." Adam could tell the alien was leading to something. It was what he did. Adam didn't like it. "Once the bank is robbed, the Klin will investigate how it happened and conclude that the perpetrators must have had detailed information about the bank. They will look to see who had access to said information … and they will find me."

"There have to be others," Callie said.

"Some, but they know of my past, and my affiliation with Humans. But even without that, the Klin would not hesitate to kill a hundred people if it meant killing the single guilty party as well."

"What are you getting at, Lion/El?" Adam asked.

"I am getting at two million energy credits for the schematics. It is evident that once the bank is attacked, I must leave the Devil's Gate. I must have the resources to do so."

"We don't have—"

Jay elbowed Adam in the ribs. Annoyed, Adam glared at the young man, until he read his expression. Jay nodded slightly. Adam got the message. He turned his attention back to Lion/El.

"Two million … and you'll give us the schematics?"

"Nothing less."

"Okay, it's a deal."

"But I will only give them to you once I have the credits in hand."

"Where, on Arancus or Josilin-Bor?"

"Arancus, of course. You are coming this way. And I suggest you hurry if you wish to beat the Clan to the bank."

"Where and when?"

"I will relay the coordinates." Lion/El laughed. "I should also ask for a share of the proceeds; I would, if I thought you would succeed. But I have seen the bank. It will be a challenge, even for you, Cain-mis."

"We'll see. You should know better than to bet against the Humans."

"There was a time when I would have agreed with you. But many things have changed recently. It is a different galaxy than during our Navarus days. I will take the credits and bet on a sure win. I will bet on myself leaving the Devil's Gate before the fireworks begin."

15

Adam was already in a hurry to pull the bank job, not wanting to spend too much time in the Devil's Gate before Tidus noticed. This thought kept rumbling around in his head, even as Adam reminded himself that if they were successful he wouldn't need his damn job at Starfire Security. But from past experience he couldn't count his chickens before they hatched. You know, the best laid plans and all that bullshit. And he was still concerned about the kill switch which he hadn't found yet.

And now with the Clan going after the bank as well, there was even more urgency.

The space within the Gate was weird, stranger than any place Adam had been in the Milky Way. The fabric of space/time was bent and twisted in a confused mess influenced by the local black holes, the stars that orbited them and the massive amount of nebular gas that surrounded the area. This made travel extremely slow, as least relatively. The six-hour journey to Arancus seemed like an eternity, causing Adam's frustration to boil over several times with the others. They would snap back at him, saying the Clan was experiencing the same handicap. Even so, the Kracori still had at least a nine-hour head start. They could be on Arancus already. Even so, could the scaly grey creatures come up with a plan that fast? Could it already be a done deal even before Adam and the others arrived on the planet? He had no way of knowing.

Even so, Adam was planning ahead, for their escape from the Devil's Gate. While riding the weird eddies and gravity pools on the way to Arancus, Adam deployed a series of magnetic mines from the *Arieel* and set along a pre-determined path. Should anyone follow them off the planet after the robbery—be they Klin or Kracori—he would lead them into the minefield to slow them down. Adam would know where the mines were laid, but not the enemy. It might give them the edge they would need to reach the Gate.

The Gate itself was another issue. During the transit, Adam recorded every detail of the route and then fed it into the autopilot. In a worst-case scenario, they would run the Gate without a pilot leading them and hope for the best. It would cause a lot of screaming and indignation from the locals, but what the hell. All they needed to do was get through the Gate and they'd be home free. The Klin were not allowed outside the Gate and there were Allied military forces stationed nearby to make sure that didn't happen. Would they care if the Klin were after them for breaking Klin law? Probably not. *Hopefully* not. Adam would cross that bridge when he came to it.

Adam had plenty of time over the past three weeks to memorize the data provided by on-site informants of General Oakes, natives on the payroll of the Human Intelligence Services. There was quite a bit here, although he had trouble discerning fact from fiction, rumor from reality. Still, there were some basic details that he came to accept based on the number of sources repeating the same stories. A plan was percolating in this brain, but he still needed a hell of a lot more information before a concrete plan could be revealed.

Upon arriving on Arancus, Adam and General Oakes were out the hatch before the hull cooled and into a rented transport to meet with Lion/El. They had the two million in counterfeit energy credits with them, which nearly cleaned out their cache. If Lion/El tried to play games and demanded more ... well, let's just say Adam was in no mood for renegotiations.

It was a strange place the alien asked the Humans to meet him: In front of the provincial police headquarters within the capital city of Boor. Although it was run by natives, there were still plenty of Klin around. Adopting the Clan's practice of cloaking and hooding up, the two Humans did the same. But just having this many of the silver-skinned bastards around made Adam anxious. He knew why Lion/El chose this spot. Any physical attack on the purple creature would surely be noticed and the authorities called in. Even simply pointing out that there were Humans here would be enough to attract an unwanted crowd and lead to their arrest.

The Lip'polin had a datapad in his hand and a satchel over his shoulder.

"Cain-mis, it is good to see you in person. As I said, your transformation is startling. I wish I knew more about what happened ... but I will save that for another day."

"Good idea," said Adam impatiently. "Now, where are the schematics?"

"Where are the credits?"

Oakes dropped the bag of credits on the grass. The obese alien knelt next to it and opened the flap. He reached one of his four hands inside and began withdrawing the thin, credit-card-size chips. He began counting them, this time employing all four of his arms, and placing them into his satchel when he was done.

"You're going to count them … *here*?" Adam asked incredulously.

"Another time would be too late."

"Don't you trust us?"

Lion/El looked up, first at General Oakes and then at Adam. "No, I do not." He went back to counting.

Feeling self-conscious and fully exposed in the middle of the greenbelt, in front of a major police station, and as a round, purple skinned alien counted out two million energy credits in plain view, Adam and Todd kept an eye out for any undue attention. It was subtle, but it was there. Several natives were in the park, enjoying the sunshine and a mid-day meal, and with the time to observe those around them. It wasn't hard for them to see Lion/El pulling prodigious amounts of credits from the bag and transferring them to his. It wasn't something the natives saw every day. They began to pay attention, as it took almost fifteen minutes for the alien to finish counting the total.

"You are short by three hundred credits."

Adam's mouth fell open. "Bullshit. It's all there."

Lion/El shrugged and reached into his now full bag of credits. "Then I shall count them again."

"No!" Oakes cried out a little too loudly. He reached into his pocket and pulled out a handful of chips. He counted out three one-hundred-credit chips and handed them to the alien. "Here, take these. That should do it."

Lion/El took the credits. Then he stood and hooked the heavy bag of credits over his shoulder. He didn't appear to struggle with the weight, telling Adam that he was stronger than the Human realized. Then Lion/El handed the datapad to Oakes.

"Check it, Todd," Adam said with a smirk. "Make sure the schematics are in there."

Lion/El smirked back.

Oakes pulled up the file and then showed the screen to Adam.

"I threw in a bonus," Lion/El said. "A guard schedule for the coming five days. I suggest you launch your operation within that time or else the schedules will change."

Adam and Oakes turned to leave.

"I get no thanks for the bonus?"

Adam flipped off the alien as they walked away.

"I do not understand the significance of the gesture," Lion/El said. "Even so, I will return it to you in the spirit it was delivered."

He flipped off the Humans using all four of this plump purple hands.

Back at the *Arieel*, Jay copied the schematics and loaded them into five separate datapads, one for each team member. Lion/El's file turned out to be more of a treasure trove than they expected. Coupled with the information they got from Unonen, along with General Oakes' initial intelligence report, Adam finally had enough to come up with an effective attack strategy. The team huddled around the coffee table in the common room as Adam laid it out for them.

"All right, I see now why you guys were so anxious to go after this target." He pointed to the schematic that was displayed on a big monitor laid flat on the table. "Security here is a joke. Having said that, here is our target, this barbell-shaped building, with two square sections connected by a long office concourse. From end to end, the building is about two thousand feet long by five hundred wide. To give you some idea of scale, the smaller connecting section is still a hundred feet wide by five stories tall, making these two end pieces pretty substantial buildings. But as you can see, the entire complex is located in the middle of a business district with no perimeter wall. We have videos provided by the General's spies, but later today we'll take a survey of the actual structure. We'll also do a trial run of the route back to the spaceport.

He ran his finger along the lower section of the block structure to the west side of the complex. There was a green dot on a large room facing south. "According to the schematics, this is where the vault is located. It's basically just a big room. Callie, fill us in on what you've learned about the security measures."

"You're right; security here is a joke." The redhead had a sinister grin on her face, excited by the prospect of another major con in the works. "From what I've learned, the bank was built at a time when the Klin occupied this part of the town. With only Klin around, it was more like a storage locker than a bank. Hell, they don't even have security cameras. Since Klin don't steal from other Klin, there was no need. The original intent was for the Klin to assimilate into the native population as a way to protect themselves against a massive Allied attack. Later, when an unofficial peace broke out between the parties, the Klin began migrating to the east, to a large enclave about ten miles east called Sylox and made up almost exclusively of Klin. Mingling with the natives no longer seemed that appealing to them.

"Even after the migration, they never upgraded the security for the building. As I said, Klin don't steal from Klin, and none of the people in the Devil's Gate had the balls to do it either, and over the years, the Klin have grown even more complacent.

"According to Lion/El's guard schedule, there are only twelve Klin standing posts at any given time. There *are* workers on site, but they remain here and here." She pointed to the west and east ends of the two block buildings. "The guards work in pairs and rotate stations every forty minutes."

She pointed to an area along the south side of the left-hand block. "Along the side of the building here, is a loading dock. It's covered by a short awning to protect against the weather. Access to the building is through these three roll-up doors. Once inside, there's a fifty-foot-wide open area before reaching the vault door."

"Jay, what about the door?" Adam asked. "Any trouble?"

Jay shook his head. "No problem. It *is* a security door but it appears to be electronically controlled through a pad on the door. By what I've seen of the circuits, it works by either applying power to the circuit or not. We can bypass the pad by cutting the wires … here." He pointed to a spot on a side wall while smiling. "And yes, this place is a joke. I told you all we had to do is waltz right in and take the money."

"That may be so, but we still have the Clan to contend with," Adam reminded him. "They're the unknown factor at the moment. And that's why we go tomorrow morning, right after rush-hour traffic has thinned. Here's how we'll do it. All of us will have suppressed nine mils and be hot-mic'ed for comms. Mike and I will drive the two trucks we'll rent this afternoon up to the loading dock as if we belong there. When the guards come out to check on us, we'll take them out, pulling the bodies back into the building. Callie and Todd will take up guard positions just inside the roll-up doors while Jay, Mike and I go into the vault."

"So, you have the girl and the old man stand guard duty while the three big, strong men do all the heavy lifting," Callie said with indignation. Then she grinned. "I'm okay with that."

Adam smirked. "From what the sources say, the credits are kept in what are called 458 security containers, and thanks to the trusty Galactic Library, we happen to know a lot about these crates. They're approximately three feet wide by four feet long and two feet deep. Comparing them to a recent experience Callie and I have with how much a container like this can hold, it's about five million credits, depending on the denomination."

Callie opened her mouth to protest.

"I know, Callie," Adam said. "Mada's container had ten million credits in it. But it was just a normal shipping container. These are security crates. They have additional locking mechanisms and climate control and they're made of metal. I've worked the numbers, fully loaded the maximum is five million.

And if there is five hundred million credits in the vault, and each crate can carry five million credits, we're talking about a hundred crates. They'll fit in the trucks with no problem. It's the *Arieel* that's the problem. I've taken some measurements, and if we fill up the cargo bay, the staterooms and the common room, they'll fit. The five of us will have to crowd into the cockpit for the six-hour flight to the Gate, but I don't think anyone will complain considering the cargo we'd be hauling. And then once we get through the Gate and back to Lo'roan, we'll have plenty of room using the *Farragut*."

"Or maybe we'll just buy a luxury liner to hold our booty, complete with a buffet and turn-down service," Mike said, grinning.

Adam shrugged and then looked to General Oakes. "I'm thinking we'll be pretty fast loading the crates into the trucks, but it's going to take longer getting them into the *Arieel* and stowed away. And we may be pressed for time at that point. Can you round up a crew of your local assets to help with the loading? Tell them we'll give them a few thousand credits each."

"*A few thousand credits* for a few minutes loading a spaceship!" Jay exclaimed. "Hell, I'll do it for that much."

"It's the *time* I'm worried about, Jay, not the money. After we hit the bank, I want to be off planet in forty-five minutes or less."

Adam looked at the anxious faces around the

coffee table. They were beaming, each ready for the operation to get underway.

"Okay, let's head over to the bank and have a look while we still have the light. I'm anxious to see this beast up close and personal."

The team carefully timed the drive to the bank, checking traffic flow, regulation lights and the presence of law enforcement. It seemed pretty straightforward. The spaceport was nine miles away and the bank could be accessed exclusively by surface streets, although alien freeways—called *ribbons* on most worlds—were available in the area. But the most direct route was on the city streets.

Adam breathed a sigh of relief when he spotted the oddly shaped building without a wall of yellow police tape surrounding the crime scene. That meant the Clan had not acted, not yet. And with his mission planned for the next morning, there was a pretty good chance they would beat the Kracori to the punch.

The bank was a prominent feature in the business district, with wide roads bordering all four sides. Adam was behind the steering stick of the transport and slowed as they passed the loading dock and roll-up doors leading to the vault. This part of the building was in full view of the roadway and anyone walking along the sidewalk. That could be a problem.

"We'll have to be careful when we take out the guards," Adam stated. "We don't want anyone to see us from the street." No guards were seen on the loading dock at the moment, but according to the schedule, they still had a half an hour before their next rotation.

Adam turned right at the west end of the building and made another circuit, with Callie shooting video for later review. The details of Adam's plan had to be confirmed and the lay-of-the-land embedded in the minds of the team. Again, it seemed almost too easy. But Adam knew there was no such thing as *'too'* easy. Even so, he was cautiously optimistic.

The next hour was spent meticulously planning the route back to the spaceport. There could be no delays, no second guessing. To that end, Adam tried three different routes, asking what would happen if this road was blocked or the Klin came at them from this street or another. The trucks would be loaded to bear with armament, so they could fight if they had to. But if it came to that, their prospects wouldn't look too good. They'd be on the planet Arancus, deep behind enemy lines and with an alerted Klin population after them. He'd planned for the possibility of pursuit but not until later, once they got into space, and not on the ground and miles from the spaceport.

During the tour of the bank and the surrounding area, they kept an eye out for the Clan or any cluster of aliens paying undue attention to the bank. All was clear, as far as they could tell. That didn't help to calm Adam's nerves. He knew the Kracori were out there somewhere, doing the same thing he was doing—planning a bank robbery. What he sincerely hoped for was that he was a little bit faster at the planning stage. So far, that seemed to be true. And according to Lion/El, Adam and his people had the guard schedule, which the Clan did not. This allowed the Humans to plan the heist without having to physically track the guard's movements to learn their routine. The Clan would have to do that if they wanted to have any chance of pulling off the heist. They may be the mighty Clan of the Hood, but here in the Devil's Gate, they faced the same hazards as did the Humans—namely the fucking Klin.

That thought brought a modicum of relief to Adam's troubled mind. If the guard schedule had to be tracked, that could easily add a day or two to the Clan's operation. Also, as far as the Kracori knew, the Humans didn't have the schematics, and without them, there could be no mission. The Clan may not feel the same urgency as did the Humans.

Yeah, this might be okay, Adam thought. They'd only been on the planet for a day, and the next morning they were hitting the bank. That had to be some kind of record for this kind of operation.

But still, there were no guarantees, and Adam had a night ahead of him to spend worrying if he'd thought of everything. Unfortunately, he wouldn't know until it was too late.

16

Two black, hard-sided trucks sat outside the *Arieel*, having been rented the day before and loaded with weapons during the evening hours, while also leaving plenty of room for the crates of energy credits.

No one ate breakfast that morning but they did chug down gallons of coffee. By Day-4—four hours after sunrise (star-rise, to be precise)—the team was chomping at the bit to get started. But they had to wait for the morning traffic to lessen and then time their arrival for after a shift change by the guards. According to the data Lion/El provided, the guards moved in a clockwise rotation around the building every forty minutes, starting at the entrance on the western façade, and then moving around the building, with each pair checking in before the relieved unit could move to their next station. It staggered the actual time of the rotation some, but not by much. Adam had to believe the schedule was a little laxed anyway. These were Klin warriors assigned to mundane security duties at a building that didn't need any, at least according to the Klin higher ups. They had to be some of the more simple-minded Klin and bored out of their narrow silver skulls by now. Today things were going to get a little more exciting, the day they earn their pay.

The trucks set off from the spaceport with Adam driving one of them and Mike Hannon the other. Jay was with Adam while Callie and Todd rode with Mike. Each of the Humans had suppressed Sig Sauer nine-millimeter semi-automatics tucked into holsters under their full-body cloaks. They also had hoods to cover their faces. This wasn't unusual on Arancus since most of the population belonged to a religious sect where the priests wore such garments. But the priests weren't known to drive heavy black trucks very often, and none were female, although it was hard to tell Callie's sex through the cloak and hood. Fortunately, no one paid them any attention on the drive to the bank. They arrived just after nine in the morning.

Adam and Mike pulled their trucks up to the loading dock and backed them up until they touched the rubber fenders. Two minutes passed, and when no one came out to question who they were and what they wanted, Adam wasn't sure what to do. He didn't want his cloaked team to try to gain access through what were undoubtedly locked roll-up doors looking for the guards. He preferred they come to him.

He looked around the truck's cab for anything that would signify a horn but found nothing.

Oh, what the hell, he thought. *This is ridiculous.*

"Everyone stay put, I'll go knock on the door."

Adam climbed out of the cab and hopped onto the loading dock before approaching one of the three doors. He banged on the metal and then waited, his hand tucked under the cloak and gripping the Sig Sauer. He even tried lifting the panel and it wouldn't move.

He stepped back suddenly when he heard a click on the other side of the door and it began to move up. Cinching the hood tighter over his head, he waited as the door opened. Fortunately for him—and not for them—both guards stood on the other side. Adam tensed slightly; it had been a while since he'd been this close to a Klin. They frowned at him, knowing him to be a priest—a very short priest—and wondering what he was doing there. One of the guards looked past him at the two trucks, raising his curiosity level even more.

"State your business, priest. You are not allowed here."

Adam turned his body sideways to the guards, waving one hand at the trucks while extracting the suppressed nine-millimeter with the other. Two quick poofs and the deed was done. Adam was dragging the bodies past the doorway as the rest of the team took up positions.

Callie and Oakes scooted just inside the door with their weapons at the ready while Mike and Jay did a quick clearing of the fifty-foot-deep interior staging area. There was no one else around. Adam joined Jay as he moved to the section of the side wall where he would access the vault door circuits.

As indicated on the schematics, the wall was made of a sheetrock-like material and Jay used a utility knife to cut away a section. Inside, he found the lead wires; they weren't difficult to decipher and he quickly sliced them with his knife.

Mike was at the vault door, which was operated by a single metal bar that would either insert or extract thick metal rods into the side panel, depending on whether or not the mechanism was energized or not. Without power to the lock, Mike was able to lift the bar and extract the rods. Real high-tech, in Adam's opinion.

Mike pulled on the heavy door, and it silently swung open.

Callie and Todd were looking back at the others, curious if they could see the treasures inside the vault. They couldn't. The lights were off inside.

Adam was the only one who came equipped with a flashlight. Mike, Jay and he entered the vault while Adam scanned the inner wall for a light switch with his beam. Jay found the switch first on an opposite wall.

"I got it," he reported, and suddenly the room was bathed in light.

The three Humans stood frozen in place for several seconds as banks of overhead lights snapped on throughout the vast room.

"What do you see?" Callie asked through the comm. "Is it there?"

When no answer came, she and Todd sprinted over to the vault door and looked inside.

"What the hell is this?" Callie asked. "This isn't right."

17

"No shit," Mike said reverently, his voice echoing lightly off the metal walls of the vault. "Are you sure we have the right place?"

Adam wasn't sure. The room was huge, belying the sterile scale of the schematics. And there *were* security crates stacked about. But rather than the hundred or so they were expecting ... the room was filled with hundreds, if not thousands, of the containers, stacked to the ceiling and as far back as they could see.

"There's a hell of a lot more than half a billion energy credits in here," General Oakes whispered. "Ten billion, maybe more."

"Why do they have so many?" Adam asked.

Jay snorted. "Who the fuck cares!" he cried out. "This is the goddamn motherlode!"

"We can't take them all," Adam pointed out needlessly. Although he was staring at an ungodly fortune in energy credits, somehow he didn't feel comfortable with the scenario. As Callie said, *this isn't right*.

"That's true," Jay said, responding to Adam's comment. "So let's take what we can. It will still make us richer than any of us ever imagined."

Mike laughed. "I don't know; I've have a pretty wild imagination."

"Yeah, but this is reality, buddy," Jay pointed out, slapping his friend on the shoulder. "Time to wake up and smell the money, *be-otch*!"

Adam walked up to the first row of crates.

"Maybe they're empty," he stated, causing a tightening in the stomachs of the team members. He lifted one of the crates. They would be heavier than normal shipping crates because of the metal construction and security features. Even so, this sucker was heavy, even for a Human. It definitely had something in it. A lot of something. He shook it as best he could and heard the tinkling plastic chips shifting inside. He'd heard the sound before. These were energy chips.

Jay and Mike hurriedly checked another eight crates at random. They couldn't open them but they could feel the weight and hear the familiar tinkle.

"We're in business!" Mike announced with a lecherous grin.

After a sigh of relief, the team set to work. As

hoped for, there were wheeled carts in the vault and the staging area used for transporting the security crates throughout the building, a lot of carts for a lot of credits. Each of them could carry four crates, and as a giddy Callie Morrison and Todd Oakes resumed their guard positions, Mike, Adam and Jay grabbed carts and began loading.

Adam couldn't help but mentally count as he did so. Each crate could hold approximately five million ECs, so each load of the cart was worth twenty million credits.

Damn! What a great way to make a living, he thought. A quick glance at the expressions of the others told him they were each thinking the same thing.

With bubbling enthusiasm, they began wheeling the carts out of the vault and to the now open backs of the trucks. They couldn't run once they got through the roll-up door; there were natives and even a few Klin walking the streets outside and driving by in transports. Adam checked his watch on the way back for another load. Thirty-one minutes until shift rotation. That should be plenty of time.

But then he started thinking about logistics. The *Arieel* could only hold so many crates. He'd already estimated that a hundred crates—the original half a billion credits—would nearly fill the starship from stem to stern. To help speed the loading and distribution of the crates within the starship, Todd had a small crew of helpers waiting at the spaceport to help. Could they possibly squeeze in a few more? And even if they could, there was the weight issue. In space, it wouldn't be a problem, but getting off the surface could be.

Surprisingly, Adam began to feel melancholy by the time he was making his fourth trip, disappointed that they would be leaving literally billions of credits on the table. The trucks would easily carry three hundred crates if stacked carefully. With a maximum capacity of the *Arieel* at a hundred crates, Adam instructed the team to just wheel the carts in and leave them loaded before going back for another cart and another load. That was well and good—for the original hundred crates. But, still, that was a hell of a lot of money to leave behind. It made him sick to his stomach thinking about it.

Adam had just loaded his fifth cart when another thought suddenly popped into his head.

Where the hell did the Klin get so many damn energy credits?

He'd been making revised counts of the rows he could see extending to the back of the vault and was already at a revised count of twenty billion, double the general's initial guess. And it could easily be twice that. His head hurt from all the calculations. There was always the possibility that most of the crates in the vault were empty, but so far, everything the team had loaded was full. It didn't matter in the end. It just would have made Adam feel better if all except a hundred crates were empty. Then he wouldn't feel so cheated.

But hell, even the *Farragut* couldn't carry this many crates. At the conversion rate from the now-obsolete Juirean credits to energy credits, a potential forty billion was more than the wealth of a dozen average tech level worlds of the former Expansion. And it could all be sitting in this one room, and in cash.

But then again: *Where the hell did they get so many credits?*

Granted, the Klin nearly conquered the galaxy, ravaging a thousand worlds and leading to the collapse of both the Juirean Expansion and the Human Orion-Cygnus Union. They would have had access to untold wealth on these conquered planets.

But then another thought crossed Adam's confused mind: Energy credits didn't even come into vogue until *after* the Klin invasion failed.

Suddenly, Adam's stomach did a somersault, and he stopped loading his cart. Instead, he examined the locking mechanism on a crate. Not seeing any simple way of opening the container without the key, he began tugging on the lid in a mad rush, hoping his Human strength would break the lock. The others saw what he was doing.

"What the hell, Adam?" Mike said. "We don't have time for sightseeing. As Kenny Rogers said, they'll be time enough for counting when the dealin's done." He looked over at Jay and grinned. "Not bad, huh? I should have been a singer."

"Not hardly," Jay grunted. "You're a better alien assassin, and at that, you're only adequate."

Adam ignored them, but when he pulled his Sig Sauer from under his cloak and pointed it at the lock, the other two Humans stopped their banter.

"What's wrong with you, Adam? We don't have time for this." Mike yelled. This time he was serious.

Adam fired.

The muffled explosion echoed off the metal walls of the room.

The locking mechanism shattered, and Adam lifted the freed lid and tossed it away in a fit of anger ... and fear.

"What are you guys doing in there?" Todd asked over the comm. "Twelve minutes and counting. Step on it."

But now Jay, Mike and Adam were huddled around the open crate, their mouths open, eyes wide, each barely breathing.

Because within the container—in all their colorful splendor—were thousands upon thousands of ... worthless *Juirean* credits.

"No ... fucking ... way." Jay whispered. "This can't be."

Adam and Mike said nothing, as they moved to two more crates and used their weapons to snap open the crates only to find more JC's.

Callie and Todd once again abandoned their posts and ran into the vault to see what the delay was. The others hadn't come out of the vault with a cart for five minutes, and they were growing nervous.

What they found was a tangible thickness in the air, one of tension and letdown. They looked into a crate, and then over at another.

"Are they all like this?" Callie asked breathlessly.

Adam shrugged. "Who knows, but I wouldn't bet against it."

"Why do they have so many?" Jay asked.

General Oakes sighed and shook his head. "In a way, it makes sense. These are the Juirean credits the Klin took from their conquered worlds during the invasion," Todd surmised. "It looks as if we broke into a storage locker full of the shit the Klin don't want."

"Yeah, well, we don't want them, either!" Mike yelled. "These things aren't worth the plastic they're printed on."

"This doesn't make any sense," Jay said. "Now we're really screwed."

"Everyone calm down," Adam ordered, although no one wasn't calm, just pissed off.

Adam's mind was a flurry of activity. "Jay's right, this doesn't make sense. The Klin still buy supplies, and they pay with ECs; all the reports say so. They have to hold them somewhere."

"Like in one of their other colonies," Mike said sourly.

Adam shook his head. "No, the reports say they're paid here, in the Devil's Gate. Some even point to this building. They have them here … somewhere. I know it."

"But where?" Todd asked. He checked his watch. "Five minutes and the next set of guards will be here. We can take them out, but then the two from here won't show up at the next station. Inquiries will be made and people will come looking for them."

"We have to bug out," Jay said. "Bug out with a couple of truckloads of worthless plastic. Maybe we can get a few hundred bucks for them at a recycling center."

Adam was in a panic. Instinctively, he knew the ECs had to be somewhere in the building, but it was a damn big place. Callie had the same thought and had her datapad out, studying the schematics. Adam stepped up to her and peered over the top of the datapad. Looking at the drawing from this angle, the truth suddenly came to him.

"I know where the money is!" he announced in a tone that left no question as to its validity.

"Where?" Mike questioned.

Adam reached over the datapad and pointed. "There."

He kicked himself mentally for not seeing it before, but he had no reason to. The part of the building they were in now was marked with a dot on the schematics. *A damn dot.* Looking back at it now, what the hell did the dot mean? He assumed it meant the vault was here. It did; there *is* a vault here. It just wasn't the right vault.

"It's in the second vault."

The team crowded in, looking at Callie's datapad.

"Look at it," Adam began. "This building is a mirror of itself, and you can see on the plans that there's another big room just like this one at the other end and on the other side of the building. We're in the wrong vault."

"The wrong vault, he says!" Jay yelled. "Like we found out we put on mismatched socks this morning. This is a big fucking deal. What are we to do now? We can't launch an assault on the other side of the building. As it is, we're about three minutes from getting our asses discovered breaking into this one. Besides, we can't be sure you're right. Your track record ain't the best."

Adam scowled at Jay. "Fine, asshole. I'll run over and take a look," Adam volunteered. "In the meantime, there are only ten live guards left in the building. If we have to, we'll take out a few more and deal with the consequences. As my good friend Jay Williford just pointed out, we're about to be found out anyway. Either we stick it out a little longer—and with a little more bloodshed—or we bug out now with nothing. Either way, the Klin are going to be on our asses in a matter of minutes. I'd rather be running away with some cash in our pockets rather than running away on empty."

"Nice speech," Callie said sardonically. "You better get moving. We'll follow in the trucks."

"I'll stay in touch on the comms."

18

Adam sprinted out of the vault while cinching the hood tighter over his head to keep it from flying off as he ran. But once outside, he had to slow his pace to a quick walk. The sight of a priest sprinting along the grounds of the Klin bank might raise some alien eyebrows. Even so, the shit was about to hit the fan. The team would probably take out the replacement guards at the first vault, but when no one showed up to relieve the pair at the western entrance, people would come looking for them. He had no idea how long that would take, but it certainly wouldn't be more than five minutes. He sighed as he walked, feeling the grip of the Sig Sauer under his cloak. No matter how he looked at it, there was gunplay in his future.

Adam had to go around the perimeter of the

eastern side of the building to reach the other side; there was no way to pass through the central 'bar' of the barbell configuration. If he'd been able to run, he could have used his Human muscles in the light gravity to make the journey in less than a minute. As it was, it took him two.

As he rounded the corner to where he could see the matching loading dock, he suddenly ducked back for cover.

There were four white vehicles backed up to the loading dock with multiple beings busy at work. Adam made out a few of the creatures; he'd seen them before: On the video in Unonen's workshop and leading to his subsequent death. They were the Clan's henchmen/beings.

"We got trouble," Adam spoke, knowing the team was listening. "The Clan is over here and they're loading up four vans. It looks like they're getting ready to leave."

"Do they have *our* money?" Jay said in Adam's ear.

"Looks like it."

"Stop them!"

Adam recoiled. "And how exactly do you suggest I do that?"

"With some of your super Adam Cain powers, that's how. Geez, that's why we brought you along."

"You asshole! Don't lay this all on me. Besides, I've

already died once; I don't want to press my luck with a second funeral."

"Jay's right, Adam," said Todd Oakes. "You're there; do something, drastic if you have to. We still have to bring the trucks around. Things are about to get a little wild around here. No time like the present to start."

"Fine, but I'd rather confront the Clan away from the bank. This is where most of the Klin in the area are located." Adam cast another glance around the side of the building. "They're packing up, getting ready to leave. I'll see if I can hitch a ride on one of the vans. We'll take them after they leave the bank. Follow my directions."

"We *have* been following your directions," Jay mocked. "That's why we're here and the Clan is over there."

"You really are an asshole, Jay."

"I learned from the best."

"Who, Mike?"

"No, *you* … you asshole!"

Adam set off, hugging the wall until he got closer to the landing bay. There were a few plants along the side of the building, but nothing like that decorating the native structures in the area. The Klin weren't into architectural aesthetics, but it was enough to provide Adam with a little cover. The building did, however, have drainage pipes leading from the flat roof. They were thick and anchored to the stone wall with heavy clamps placed every six feet or so along the length. They made for an effective ladder, and Adam was soon scampering toward the roof. At this point, he didn't care if people on the street noticed the priest climbing the outside of the Klin bank building. The cat was about to come screaming out of the bag and everyone in the neighborhood would hear it.

At the roof, Adam moved along until he was above the awning covering the loading dock. It was about twenty feet below him and Adam didn't hesitate to simply leap over and used his enhanced Human muscles to buffer the landing. The awning was made of concrete so there was no sound as he landed. He moved to the edge and laid down. Cautiously, he poked his head over.

The vans were still a good three feet farther under the awning, and fortunately, there was a gutter running along the edge of the awning that afforded the Human a handhold. Adam gripped the metal edge and swung over, dropping to the ground another thirty feet below.

He moved up to the front of what was the second van in the row and hid against the front grill. Most of the aliens were on the loading dock, whispering to each other and placing the last crates in the back of the vans. They began buttoning them up.

Adam hurried to the van next to him, the one at the east end of the loading dock. And then using a ledge on the windshield, he climbed the front of the van and slid onto the top, lying flat so no one would see him.

According to his *natural lines of drift* training from the SEALs, this should be the last vehicle in the caravan as they turned west toward the spaceport. Like Adam and his team, the Clan would want to get off Arancus as soon as possible.

"I'm on top of the end van," he whispered in his comm. "They'll leave here and head for the spaceport. I'll be on the trailing van. Once we pull away, give me a few minutes to move into the cab and take out whoever's in there. Then I'll call in an intercept course. We need to stop the other vans and take control of them. Be ready, they're moving into the vans now."

There was a hurried move to the vehicles by the Clan; Adam could tell by the muffled speech and sound of footfalls now moving along the length of the vehicles. Doors opened and then shut and electric engines engaged. The vans began to move.

And then Adam's heart skipped a beat. Rather than turning left and moving out onto the street leading west and to the spaceport, the vehicles turned right, toward the east. This placed Adam hugging the roof of the lead van, not the trailing van.

"Ah, fuck!" Adam whispered. "They turned east. Where the hell are they going?"

"Give me a second to check the map," Callie said in his ear.

As he waited, Adam did all he could to keep his cloak pressed against his body and not flapping in the wind. It was already a miracle he hadn't been spotted by the following vans. He had to be in just the right blind spot on the roof. But it also meant he couldn't move. Fortunately, he was laying on his stomach and able to turn his head from side to side, catching glimpses of road signs.

"I think I have something," Callie reported. "A small, private spaceport located on the fringe of the Klin enclave, about eight miles from here. That must be where they have their ships."

"Great, we're heading right into the belly of the beast," Adam groaned.

"We have to stop them soon, Adam," General Oakes said. "Where are you now? Can you tell?"

"Crap! We studied the route from the bank to the main spaceport, not this way. There are road signs, but they're all in Arancus-ese, or whatever they call themselves."

"How about unique buildings, other landmarks? All we have to do is find you then we'll map out an intercept."

Now lying on his back was a handicap. He tried to twist a little so he could look up and around. That was risky. He figured the reason he hadn't been spotted was because the vans were moving in a tight caravan and not more spread out. Either way, it was a matter of when, not if, he'd be spotted.

"There's a pointed building to the left, maybe three or four blocks over. It seems to be the only one that's pointed."

"I got it!" Callie shouted. "Yeah, nothing else like it in this part of town. Are you coming up on it or passing it?"

"We're about level with it now."

"Have they turned off the road that parallels the bank?"

"Not yet."

"Okay, I think we have you, at least enough to hurry to that point looking for the vans. What color are they?"

"White; four of them moving in a line. Not hard to miss."

"We're on our way—"

"Wait!" Adam whispered. "They're turning, turning left."

"I think we're okay," Callie said. "We have two trucks and we know their destination. I have a pretty good idea where you are. Hang in there, and don't get spotted."

"Damn, I wish I'd thought of that. Good advice."

"Glad I could help. We're speeding up to get ahead

of you. It's pissing off a lot of natives, but what the fuck, they're only aliens."

"I knew there was something I liked about you. We both have rotten attitudes when it comes to aliens."

The caravan made another turn, this time to the right, and Adam relayed the information to Callie.

"I got 'em," Mike said from one of the trucks. Jay was with him, Oakes with Callie. "They're ahead of me about two blocks."

Todd was driving the heavy truck that followed Mike's, while Callie tracked their movement on her datapad.

"It looks as if they may stay on this road for a while. Todd, shift over to the parallel road. We'll try to get ahead of them."

"The traffic is heavier," the general pointed out as all parties were in stop and go traffic, working eastward through a series of stop lights. Civilized society couldn't function with chaos being the rule rather than the exception. So, even on alien worlds there were traffic jams and signal lights.

Todd turned at the next intersection, moving the beast of a vehicle along tight roads filled with much smaller cars. And he wasn't subtle about it. He crowded cars out of the way, even jumping the curb now and then to squeeze by. At one point, he forced his way through a red light, enlisting a chorus of screeching sounds that passed for horns on Arancus.

"We're almost there, Adam," Callie said. "A couple more blocks and we'll be ahead of you. We'll try to sandwich the vans between our trucks."

"Please hurry," Adam said. "There's a truck next to me and the people inside are pointing. This is about to get really bad."

19

Adam had his head turned toward the truck which sat higher than normal traffic. The driver had seen him on the roof the moment he pulled up and came to a stop at the light. It was strange enough to see someone riding on top of the van, but a priest? The driver couldn't ignore that.

He gestured to the people in the cab of the van and then pointed to the roof. It wasn't too cryptic, and Adam sensed the Clan members got the message right away because when traffic began moving, the van didn't.

Instead, both the driver and passenger doors opened and a pair of aliens jumped out and moved away from the van. One jumped on the hood of another car so he could see on top of the van.

Adam didn't have a choice. He rolled over and sat

up, the hood still pulled tightly over his head. The moment's hesitation, as the bad guy was more confused by the priest on the roof rather than alarmed, was time enough for Adam to place a nine-millimeter slug into his forehead. Adam then spun around and sighted the passenger alien. He had an MK-17 in hand and was bringing it to firing position. He didn't get a chance before Adam took him out with a shot to center mass.

By then, the aliens in the trailing vans were leaving their vehicles and aiming their weapons. Adam slid over the side and ducked into the cab just as a pair of flash bolts streamed by the doorway. He was in a sitting position a moment later and pressing the control stick forward, sending the van racing through the intersection.

Fortunately, because the Clan had stopped their vehicles, blocking traffic from behind, there were no transports in the intersection. Adam raced away—for about a block—before he caught up with the traffic going east.

That didn't stop him. He twisted the control stick to the right and jumped a curb, using the sidewalk to make a turn at the next intersection. Yellow-skinned natives did their best to jump out of his way, but being aliens, most didn't make it. He didn't run them over, but rather not-so-gently pushed them out of the way.

And then he steered back on the street and began weaving his way through slightly lighter traffic.

Just then, a sliding window from the cab to the back of the van opened and the barrel of an MK poked through. The weapon discharged nearly point-blank next to Adam's right shoulder. The plasma bolt burnt through the clothing and singed his skin before splashing against the dashboard. Fortunately, neither Adam nor the van's electronics were affected much. Adam twisted and began spraying hot lead from his Sig Sauer into the back of the van. He had no idea how many aliens were back there, but he emptied the magazine before pulling the weapon back and fenagling another mag into the gun. He sent a couple more rounds into the back, hoping the threat was neutralized or was too scared to come out from behind one of the security crates in the rear.

"I'm in the van, still heading east," Adam reported through his comm. "Where are you?"

"Now following," Callie reported. " The other three vans are on your tail. Mike is behind them; we're trying to get back on the main road. What now?"

"Get to the spaceport, our spaceport."

"What about the money?" Jay asked.

"We have one of the vans. The others will follow, I'm sure. We'll take them at the port."

"Okay, that sounds like a plan," Jay conceded. "But

it's now ten miles through city traffic to get to the spaceport."

"Just try to stay with me. I'm turning now, getting back on the road that leads back to the bank."

"Is that a good idea?" Callie asked.

"It's the way I'm most familiar with. Hopefully, the Clan assholes won't be. Just don't be too far behind. If they manage to stop me, I might like a little back up."

The van was easier to maneuver through city traffic than was the truck, and Adam managed to stay ahead of the pursuit by recalling his days driving on the freeways of Southern California. Every few blocks, he'd stick the barrel of the Sig Sauer through the window and pop off a round, just to keep anyone who might be back there honest. He could see through the rearview camera at the other vans. They were doing their best to keep up but trying to outrace a Human through traffic was a lost cause.

Soon he approached the Klin bank again and had to slow down. There was a lot more traffic here, being bunched up because of police activity at the building. It was just being set up, and Adam smirked as he passed the loading dock on the east end of the building. The dock was filled with Klin and a mixture of natives. Adam checked his watch. It had only been fifteen minutes since he left the bank, making the response much quicker and efficient than expected. Jay was right; they would not have had time to hit the second vault before the place would have been swarming with yellow- and silver-skinned bastards.

Adam was waved through and the police officer even gave him a stylized bow as he past, a tribute to the priesthood. Adam didn't know how to respond so he simply nodded. It seemed to work.

"Be careful around the bank," he said over the comm. "The Klin are out in force and someone might recognize the trucks. They're not as common as the vans."

"Roger that," Oakes said. "We'll cut over to a side street. Besides, the traffic is really beginning to bottleneck as we get closer to the bank."

Adam now picked up more speed. He debated whether or not to try to lose the pursuit by doing some reckless and dangerous driving but decided against it. By now, the Clan would know he was headed for the spaceport. Even if he lost them, they'd just show up there within minutes. All he needed to do was keep them from stopping him before he got there. The general had ten of his local assets waiting to help load the *Arieel*. It was a good bet the Clan wouldn't be expecting them to be there. But then Adam had a thought.

"Hey, Todd," Adam said. "What are your people like at the spaceport? Are they fighters?"

"Hardly. Mainly natives, just eyes on the ground."

"Will they help us fight the Clan?"

"Probably, if they have no choice, and if they have weapons."

"We have the weapons aboard the ship. I can arm them if I have a couple of minutes. Can you contact them?"

"Do you think that's a good idea? It might give them the time to bug out."

"Good point." Adam laughed. "Okay, I'll make the gun battle a surprise. I'm sure they'll appreciate that."

Adam winced from pain as he sent another round into the back. His shoulder was stiffening from the flesh wound, but he knew that it wouldn't last long. With his still-cloning body, he would heal much faster than normal people and he could tolerate pain better. Even still, it always pissed Adam off when he got shot. And the day was early.

As Adam neared the spaceport, the Clan made a concerted effort to stop him. They sped up even more and tried to box him out and the four rapidly speeding vehicles raced through a stop light. Cars spun out to avoid the vans with several side collisions left in the aftermath. The Clan vehicles got tied up in the mess, although none were damaged enough to take them out of the pursuit. But it did give Adam a little breathing room, maybe a minute or two more.

Then came the entrance to the spaceport. This was a semi-secure facility, meaning people could come and go, but vehicles were restricted without clearance. That meant a gate and a security building. Since the city Boor was the capital of the planet Arancus and the home of most Klin in the Devil's Gate, the security building was big and impressive, even as the gate was thin and more a symbol than an actual barrier.

Adam paid the barrier, as well as the lingering guards, little attention as he blasted through the gate, splintering it into a thousand pieces. This upset the guards to no end and more rushed out of the building to survey the scene and the damage. They were still in a rage of indignation when they had to dive out of the way of the other three vans that plowed through the crowd three minutes later. But this time the guards were more prepared. They fired their weapons at the speeding vehicles, managing to slow them down by a few seconds more.

Adam snickered, knowing the future and how in a few minutes, two huge black trucks would also run the entry gate. This was a day that would be talked about in the security office for years to come.

The *Arieel* was parked to the rear of the vast, dirt-covered field that served as the spaceport. The van left a cloud of raw, brown dust as it barreled toward the starship. By Adam's estimate, he had about a three-minute lead on the enemy vans. That wasn't a lot of time to get the loading crew armed and ready but it would have to do.

Adam skidded to a halt near the rear cargo bay door and turned the vehicle sideways to give them more cover. He jumped out and approached the lounging group of alien workers who were gather at the stern of the ship. They were mainly Arancus, with a couple of odd species thrown in. They looked concerned—even bothered by the sudden arrival of the van.

"You are late," one of the larger, yellow-skinned creatures yelled. "We agreed to work for seven hundred credits each, but for our idle time, we demand more."

Adam waved his hand while fingering in the code that opened the cargo bay door. "I'll pay you a lot more if you help me."

"We have already agreed to help."

"Help me fight." He rushed into the cargo hold and ran to a bin that carried flash weapons. Teaching the aliens to use Human ballistic weapons was out of the question in the time he had. Besides, the recoil would shatter their fragile bones. He pulled out several MKs and began shoving them into the hands of the loading crew before going back for more.

"What are these for?"

"To fight off the people who are coming to kill us." Adam pointed to the large dust cloud making its way across the landing field.

The alien leader was taken aback, as were the others. "I am confused. We are not here to fight."

"Then you'll die. The ones coming here will kill everyone unless we fight back." Adam had taken an M88 out for himself and snapped a magazine into the receiver. He stuffed another two magazines into the pockets in his cloak.

The yellow alien frowned and cocked his head. "You are not a priest, are you?"

Adam threw back the hood. "No, I'm a Human."

"A Human! I have heard of your kind. What are you doing on Arancus?"

"Trying to stay alive. I suggest you do the same."

Suddenly, three of the loaders dropped their weapons and sprinted off across the spaceport. Adam saw the others getting ready to run, as well.

"Wait! I'll give you more credits, a lot more credits."

"How much?"

Adam opened the back of the van, his weapon at the ready in case there were any live Clan in the back. Instead, a bloody corpse flopped out and landed on the dirt. Adam ignored him. "These are security crates full of energy credits. I can pay you … a lot."

The vans were only a hundred yards away and were slowing, seeing more people around the *Arieel* than they were expecting. The vehicles cut sideways to the starship and screeched to a stop.

"How much in each crate?"

"Why does that matter? There's plenty in there to pay you."

"We want a crate." The alien leader looked around at the remaining five; another one had run away.

"Are you crazy. There's five million credits in a crate."

"Are our lives not worth that? And as I see, you have a lot more crates."

"Fine!" Adam yelled.

"Fine? I do not understand."

"Yes! I agree. One crate, but hurry. They're getting ready to attack."

The six loaders and Adam took up positions around the van and the *Arieel*. "I must warn you," said the leader, "but I believe none of us have ever fired an energy weapon before. I know I have not."

Adam gawked at the creature. "Not even an MK, like these? I thought everyone knew how to fire an MK."

"There has been no need."

"Okay, listen up. On the top is a dial. That's the energy setting. Everyone put their dial to the second notch. That's a Level-2. You will have ten shots, so don't waste them. And don't worry about replacing the battery. There are more weapons in the ship if you run out. Just grab another—"

Adam ducked as a barrage of flash bolts began striking the van and the side of the *Arieel*.

"And don't worry about the targeting computer. Just point and shoot."

"And we will hit something?"

"Probably not, but I have reinforcements coming; General Oakes and other Humans."

The alien nodded. He knew who Oakes was, even if he'd never met him.

The next few minutes was a study in complete chaos on the battlefield. Adam's ad hoc army did aim and shoot; however, like most aliens, they had no particular eye-hand coordination. Their shots went wild, most a foot or two off target from where they were supposedly aiming. Adam was expecting this. He didn't need them to kill the enemy, just hold them at bay until the calvary arrived.

In the meantime, Adam picked off a couple of the aliens with accurate shots from the long range M88. He tried to get a count of the force that was against him and concluded there were five aliens in each of the three vans, so fifteen shooters. And they were better shots than Adam's army.

As Adam took out another careless enemy soldier, he sighted through the scope for any of the actual Clan members, the Kracori leaders. They were there, with Xan-fi rifles and firing with more accuracy than the others. Adam knew for a fact that the Kracori were nearly the equal of Humans in the art of war, making them a formidable opponent.

And then the next shoe dropped.

A spaceport security truck came rumbling toward the firefight, the local police not content to let people break through their barrier and get away with it. Adam shrugged. These new aliens were innocents, but unfortunately they were about to be classified as the enemy in Adam's mind.

But just then, the Clan fighters called off their attack, jumped in the vans, and sped off. They were letting Adam keep the one van of energy credits, thinking that three would be enough for them—if they could get them off planet and out of the Devil's Gate.

That was Adam's concern, as well.

Adam's army was down to four fighters, and they now stopped and cheered as the white vans raced away. They remained in the open as spaceport police arrived, thinking they had come to save the day. Instead, the truck came to a stop and ten armed troops jumped out, with the lead units opening fire on Adam's hapless fighters as soon as their boots hit the ground.

"Why? Why are they shooting at us?" asked the leader as he ducked for cover. Then he looked hard at Adam. "Are *you* the villain?"

"That depends on your point of view."

"Then we will not fight for you!"

Adam eyed the other four fighters and then asked, "What's five million divided by four?"

The aliens blinked their golden eyes ... and then returned to the fight.

There wasn't much Adam and his people could do against ten trained security personnel except hold their ground until Oakes arrived. As Adam sat behind the front driver's side wheel of the van, he wondered what was taking the general so long?

The port security troops weren't anxious to rush the starship, so they stayed back. Adam and his people would occasionally light off a bolt to keep the police honest and behind their cover. The stalemate lasted another five minutes, which was an eternity in a firefight.

And then the calvary arrived. With the police distracted by the approaching trucks, Adam chanced a look around the van to see what the troops were doing. They were turning their weapons against the trucks, more out of caution than anything else. They didn't know who these people were who were crashing their party.

But then the trucks turned broadside to the security truck and the Humans jumped from the cab, four of them standing about a hundred and fifty feet away and cradling their own M88s—all except Jay Williford. He had an RPG.

A hundred and fifty feet was within the range of the police Xan-fi rifles, but anything past a hundred and they became notoriously inaccurate. Jay shot off the RPG, aimed about twenty yards to the left of the security truck. It landed with a thunderous explosion, not only scaring the shit out of the aliens, but showing also that their truck was well within range of the Human's weapon.

They didn't have to be told twice, and twenty seconds later, all the security personnel were in their vehicle and racing away.

Adam's four friends ran up to him, astounding the four surviving loaders with their phenomenal Human speed.

"That was fun," Jay said, still carrying the spent RGG launcher. He had more rockets in the *Arieel*.

"Is this the loading crew?" General Oakes said, disappointment thick in his tone.

"There were more, but some ran off and two got killed," Adam told him.

"Which one of you is Lanis, or is he one of the ones who ran away?"

"I am Lanis; you must be Oakes."

"That's right. I want to thank you for your service to the Allies for all these years, and especially for risking your life to preserve the fight against the Klin."

"We are not here for the fight; we are here for the credits."

General Oakes nodded. "Of course. Seven hundred each—"

"No. Five million."

Todd recoiled. "What are you talking about? I offered you seven hundred."

Lanis pointed at Adam. "He promised us five million … one of the crates in the carrier."

Oakes turned to Adam. "You did what? There's not that much to spare, not with a quarter of the take, if the Clan split the five hundred million equally among the vans." He looked in the open back of the van. Following the assumption of half a billion credits, divided into crates with five million credits each, there should be twenty-five crates in the back of this van. There looked to be that many … plus a dead alien on the ground and two more in the back, splayed out on the crates.

"He promised," the native repeated, standing his ground.

"I did," Adam shrugged. "Hey, I needed the fighters and was pressed for time."

"Don't give it to them!" Jay said, stepping forward with the rocket launcher still on his shoulder. Even though it was empty, the aliens backed away in fear.

"No," Adam said. "I promised, and they did risk

their lives. Two even died." Adam looked at the leader. "Be sure to give shares to the families of the dead."

Lanis nodded. "Of course," he said, but Adam didn't believe him.

The Human stepped up to the much taller alien. "Be sure you do it, or else I'll know … and I'll come back and kill you." He looked at the others and waved a finger at them. "I'll kill *all* of you."

"That was a harsh reaction," Lanis said. "I said I would do that, and I will."

"Good. And nothing for the cowards who ran away. Now, you have some other work to do. My friends will help and tell you where to put the crates. And hurry. We've dealt with the Clan and port security. Next up will be the Klin. And trust me, they won't be running away once they show up."

Everyone set to work like they had a purpose, including the Humans, everyone except Adam who had to prep the *Arieel* for liftoff. There would be no permission granted from the tower or flight plan issued. The Klin would know that their stolen credits were headed off planet, making the spaceport there logical target. And the spaceship where a couple of firefights just happened would be a good place to start the search.

But before doing anything, Adam pulled a crate from the working party carrying them into the starship. He set it on the ground, took out his Sig, and blasted open the lock. Everyone paused nervously as he pulled back the lid.

Energy credits, thousands of them, in all their colorful glory. And in hundred chip denominations, the most common.

Adam's heart calm down; it had been pounding in his throat seconds before. One part of him was expecting the worse, while the optimist in him had fingers and toes crossed. Surely, the Clan checked before loading the crates into the vans. But he had to be sure.

"This crate is for you," he said to Lanis. "Spend it wisely. Fortunes like this don't come around very often." And boy, did he know it.

20

The loading of the crates took longer than expected, which made sense considering that the civilian loading team was four individuals rather than ten. But the Humans did more than the aliens by a factor of two, and soon the crates were stacked and secured. There ended up being twenty crates after giving one to the natives. So, that was a little less than the twenty-five they were expecting. Hell, it was an estimate anyway, but close enough. If all the crates held five million energy credits—and that was a big 'if' as well; no one had counted the actual amount—then they had an even hundred million credits. That was a lot of money, until you divided it by five. That left only twenty million each. As Adam prepped the ship, he was kicking himself for feeling so depressed. Sure, he'd been expecting a cool one hundred twenty-five million when it was just Jay, Mike, Todd and him. Adding Callie didn't seem like such a big deal when they were talking about that much money. Now, even the loss of one crate to Lanis dropped each of their net by a million. As they say, a million here, a million there, and pretty soon you're talking about some real money. Of course, that was a politician talking about billions of dollars. But to scale, it was the same thing to Adam.

It certainly changed Adam's attitude about a great many things, the least of which was his employment with Starfire Security. Initially, having a hundred and twenty-five million would have bought his freedom for the rest of his life. What that meant, he wasn't sure. He couldn't imagine himself doing nothing for decades as his reborn body slowly aged. But it would certainly take off some of the pressure, as well as buy him a bunch of neat shit.

But with only twenty million, it wasn't enough to last him the rest of his life. He would still have to work, which he would do anyway. Maybe he'd start his own security company; he'd already done the bar and grill route and that hadn't been as much fun as he imagined. And he wasn't that much into travel—hell, he'd traveled farther than any Human—ever—and to some really weird places. As a result, it took a lot to impress him these days.

Adam sighed and began the pre-launch countdown. He had to accept reality: He was addicted to the thrill, to the adrenaline rush. It was why he volunteered for the SEAL program and made it through the torture that was BUD/S training. It was also why he was still in space rather than back on Earth. It was a big planet; he could have surely found a quiet place where people would leave him alone. So, it came down to the rush, to challenge, to the variety of a life chasing bad guys throughout the galaxy.

But damn, twenty million was a far cry from one hundred twenty-five. Then he asked himself: Would he have even gone on the mission if the potential payout had been twenty mil instead of a hundred and twenty-five? He laughed, remembering a scene from the movie *The Magnificent Seven*, where Steve McQueen relates the story of a guy who took off all his clothes and jumped on a cactus. When asked why he did it, the guy replied: "It seemed like a good idea at the time."

"All loaded and buttoned up," Callie said as she came into the cockpit. She took the co-pilot's seat and strapped in. At one time, the team was to crowd into the cockpit for the journey back to Lo'roan since the rest of the ship would be filled with security crates. But with only a quarter of what was expected, everything ended up fitting in the cargo hold.

Adam gave her a sick grin, which she returned. No words were needed; they all felt the same way. They had something to show for their efforts, but it wasn't a lot. For her part, Callie stole twenty-five million from Bandors Bank a couple of months ago, expecting to net twelve-point-five after splitting with Mada Niac, her not-so-silent partner. Her current payout of twenty million wasn't much bigger than that.

"All right everyone, strap in," Adam announced over the ship's 1-MC system. "I'm not going to ask for permission to lift. After our little shootout with spaceport security, I doubt I'd get it. So, if it's not the Klin chasing us, it could be Arancus police. Either way, expect a bumpy ride. Okay, engaging the engines."

Adam flicked the switch … and nothing happened.

He tried it again, and again, nothing.

"What's wrong?" Callie asked.

Adam pursed his lips and gnashed his teeth before speaking. "Tidus Fe Nolan happened, that's what."

Oakes, Mike and Jay were at the cockpit entrance. They knew about the kill-switch Tidus had hidden somewhere in the ship. They'd spent a token amount of time looking for it but then gave up. They didn't feel it was that important since Tidus would never arbitrarily shutdown the *Arieel* again … would he? And especially if Adam was on a mission.

But as far as Tidus knew, Adam was through with his *official* mission. And with a way to track the ship's location, it was a good bet Tidus knew Adam was deep in the Devil's Gate. But why was he there? Tidus wouldn't release the ship until he had answers.

"Shit! I'm going to have to call him," Adam snarled.

Adam shot a killer look at the CW comm station when a link announcement came through. It had to be Tidus. And Adam hadn't had a chance to come up with a plausible explanation. He activated the link.

But it wasn't Tidus.

Thinking that it would be the Juirean, Adam allowed video conferencing with the link rather than audio only. Now, a shocked Klin official was staring not only at Adam, but the three other Humans standing behind him. Callie was in the co-pilot's seat and not visible to the Klin.

"You … you are Humans!" the alien gasped.

Having been caught, Adam just smirked. "Correct. You win a cookie."

The Klin looked down at something on either the desk or console in front of him. When he looked back up, his expression was one of pure hatred.

"Humans are restricted within the Devil's Gate. In addition, the vessel I am linking with has been implicated in not only an altercation at the spaceport, but also a theft that occurred at the Swean Holding Center earlier today. You are ordered to surrender yourselves and your vessel immediately. Security units have been dispatched, and I assure you, many more will join in the effort knowing you are Humans. Your presence is a direct violation of existing non-interference agreements."

"Sorry, slick," General Oakes said from behind Adam. "But there are no official non-interference agreements. Technically, we are still at war with the Klin. You only survive in the Gate because we let you."

The silver skin of the Klin turned a shade darker and his golden eyes burned with intensity. "I am interpreting your comment as a refusal to surrender. I accept that wholeheartedly. Now there will be no compromise. Your ship will be destroyed where it sits."

"Then so will your money—your energy credits," Mike Hannon pointed out.

"That matters not. We would gladly spend ten times more if it meant the death of Humans. Now, this conversation is over."

The screen went blank.

Adam turned and grimaced at the men behind him. "That might not have been the best tact to take, especially since we're sitting in the middle of a big open field and with a dead ship."

"Then you better get it undead," Oakes commanded. There was no ambiguity in his tone.

Adam set to work opening a CW link with Tidus back on Tel'oran. It only took a few seconds, and as expected, Tidus came on the line directly, looking angry but trying to hide it with a vial of smugness.

"I was wondering when I'd hear from you. What the fuck are you doing in the Devil's Gate?"

"Dammit, Tidus, I don't have time to explain. You picked the worst possible moment to play your power games with me. There's a force of Klin about to rain fire down on us and your precious starship. Release the kill switch so we can get out of here."

"We…" Tidus took in the three men behind him. He knew Mike Hannon but not the others. "What kind of side hustle are you involved in now, and with a total of four Humans?"

Callie leaned into view and waved. "And me, too. Hi, I'm Callie. I think Adam has mentioned me before."

"Callie … Morrison, the thief? Now, I have to hear this story."

"I'm serious, Tidus! We're about to die. Release the kill switch."

The green skinned alien pouted his lips and stared intently at Adam. "I will do it, but you better get your pink-skinned ass back here as soon as possible. And when you get clear you better link with me and give me the details of what you have been doing. I don't want to wait until you show up here, not like all the other times when you—"

"Tidus!"

"All right … there, you have control. But I'm serious—"

Adam cut the link and lit off the lifting jets simultaneously. And it was none too soon.

Two air-breathing security craft screamed over the spaceport, zeroing in on the *Arieel*. Adam had the screens up a split second before the first flash bolts struck. The ship rocked, sending Jay, Mike and Todd tumbling backwards out of the cockpit. *Good*, Adam thought. *They were getting on my nerves.*

"Strap in, assholes!' he yelled back at them, not bothering with the ship's comm system. And then he activated a shallow gravity-well.

The fighter aircraft had been expecting this and stayed back, hovering beyond the influence of the miniature blackhole. They fired again as the *Arieel* gained speed, racing for space. The shields held and the starship reached space without damage.

But they did have company.

The Klin had a pair of Mod-2 KFVs—Klin Fleet Vessels—already in space and waiting for the Human starship. This particular version of the KFV was saucer-shaped—liked the originals—but a little smaller, much faster and better armed. They were also manned by the more warrior-like Klin from the Newfound Galaxy which helped make these two starships especially lethal.

Adam increased well-intensity and shot away, with the Klin taking up the pursuit and matching speed. Adam had a little more left in reserved—it didn't pay to reveal all your capacity at the outset—but it wouldn't be enough for him to lose the pursuit. That was fine; it was almost best if the Klin remained relatively close. He was on course for the minefield he'd laid on the way to Arancus.

Even General Oakes didn't know the full capacity of the Klin forces within the Devil's Gate. The Klin arrived here with their Milky Way fleet fully intact. They only stopped fighting because they lost contact with their universe and the around-the-clock support they got from the Newfound Galaxy. Two and a half million fighters—along with their weapons of war—may sound like a lot, but not when attempting to conquer a galaxy. Wisely, the Klin stopped fighting and tried to slink off into obscurity. That was impossible; however, they did find a happy medium.

As Adam raced through space, he was wondering how far the Klin would go to stop them? Would they follow them through the Gate and risk igniting another galactic conflict? Probably not, Adam reasoned, and especially not over credits. The Klin never placed much value on money. They only had it because other races wanted it in order to trade with them. And would they risk war just to kill a few trespassing Humans? Again, hopefully not. But that didn't mean they wouldn't throw everything they had at them to stop the *Arieel* from returning to Allied space. These first two KFVs—even if Adam managed to destroy them in the minefield—certainly wouldn't be the only ones sent out to get them.

Combat between ships in gravity-wells was rare and dangerous; the singularities could be used as weapons, an unbeatable force. But most combat vessels had ways of overloading gravity-wells and dissolving the microscopic blackholes, dropping the target vessel into normal space. This is what the two KFVs were trying to do to the *Arieel*. They were flanking the starship but staying far enough away so that the wells didn't merge. Adam had been counting on this when he deployed the mines on the way in. He placed them far enough away on the outside of the course he traveled so they wouldn't be sucked up in the enemy's wells, but still close enough that the magnetics would be effective.

The problem: He only had so many mines to lay and if the Klin called in more ships, he wouldn't have enough to take them all out. And the *Arieel* was a far cry from a combat vessel. It had some weapons, including a few Adam had retrofitted. But the newer KFVs were true fighting ships. He had to make sure they didn't knock him out of the gravity-well. At that point, it wouldn't be much of a fight.

Adam had the plot screen up and was steering the

Arieel into the kill zone. The mines were marked in white so they'd standout on the screens black background. The Klin ships were also white, but with circles around them. The *Arieel* was larger and in red. Adam changed course slightly and the Klin followed. Good. Reel them in.

As the *Arieel* entered the field, Adam activated the mines. Until now, they'd been dormant—what was traditionally called *dark status*. Now that their tracking systems were active, they would stay dark until they locked onto a target. A slight nudge to the right and one of the trailing KFVs came within range of a mine.

It locked on and shot off, coming at the Klin vessel from behind so as to avoid the forward gravity-well. Magnetic mines were tiny gravity-drive ships in their own right but with such a faint signature that they would only be detected a split second before attaching themselves to the hull of the target ship. Once the first mine was locked on, Adam set about steering the second KFV close to the port side row of mines.

Adam looked over at Callie and grinned when the second Klin warship picked up a pair of mines. The first one had also acquired a second mine and all the deadly weapons were inexorably closing on their targets.

"Feeling pretty good about yourself, aren't you, Mr. Cain?" Callie said mockingly. "So, you got lucky."

"Luck had nothing to do with it, sweetheart. Skill … nothing but pure skill."

Her sarcastic voice was betrayed by the sparkle in her blue eyes. Adam knew she was impressed. All he had to hope for was that she stayed impressed. When she stopped, that would mean they were in a world of hurt.

The Klin ships detected the mines only moments before they snapped onto the metal hulls. They tried radical, ninety-degree course changes to evade the mines, but it didn't work. Once the two white contacts merged … it was all over. The *Arieel* was too far away to witness any of the explosions, but that didn't matter. The contacts disappearing from the screen told Adam and Callie all they needed to know.

The other team members had been standing back near the door to the cockpit. There was room for them in other parts of the ship since the *Arieel* wasn't packed with a full complement of security crates. But they wanted to see the action.

"What now, slick?" Callie asked. "We still have to get through the Gate."

"I have a plan for that, too," Adam said with a wink.

"Oh, yeah, I've heard of that strategy," Mike Hannon said sarcastically. Everyone knew what he had in mind. They discussed it on the way in. "They do the same thing when they used to run bulls through the streets of Paloma. Both the tourists and bulls didn't come out of that unfazed."

"They kill the bulls after the run, in the bullring, not during the run," General Oakes amended.

"And it's in Pamplona, Spain, not Paloma," Callie corrected.

Mike locked his jaw. "Okay, well screw you guys. You know what I mean."

Jay laughed. "Yeah, it means you don't know what the hell you're talking about."

"Have you even heard of the Running of the Bulls festival?" Mike asked Jay. "You're like twelve years old, aren't you?"

"Not quite, but I'm still in my prime, old man."

"Hey, watch what you say, Jay," General Oakes said. "I resemble that remark."

Adam snickered. "So do I."

"Not hardly, asshole," Mike said for the team. Each member would give their eye teeth to be reborn as their twenty-two-year-old selves as Adam had been. Even Jay. Of course, they would have to die first. That was always the clincher in any discussion they had about Adam's fateful cloning.

Todd Oakes pointed at the screen. "More incoming; they're coming from the security stations near the Gate. I don't think the bastards want us to go through."

"Go strap in," Adam said seriously. "We can't

outfight them, so we'll have to outmaneuver them. It's going to get bumpy."

There were four ships closing on their position although Adam couldn't tell what kind of vessels they were. Their gravity signals told him they were decent size, maybe Klin destroyers which were larger than the KFVs, which often served the role of large fighter craft launched from carriers or battleships during deep space operations.

The destroyers would be slower than the KFVs and less maneuverable. But there were four of them and they were blocking Adam's path to the Gate. Normal operations in space weren't so restricted. Afterall, this was space, and there was a lot of it. But the tidal gravity effects in the region made the specific transit line between the blackholes crucial. Getting past the destroyers was one thing; making it through the Gate was another.

Adam began a series of radical turns to port and then starboard, giving the Klin ships a harder target to box in. And then two of them lit off EMP missiles that cut across Adam's path and detonated. The effect was immediate as the gravity well overloaded and then dissolved. A fraction of a second later, the *Arieel* was in normal space … and a sitting duck.

21

But Adam was ready for this. He simply activated the aft gravity-well and whipped around to port, pulling the *Arieel* along with it backwards. Adam engaged the rear cameras and had to reorient himself to the controls, remembering that left was now right and vice versa. To his delight, the tactic caught the Klin off guard and they raced by on the starboard side. Once behind the *Arieel*, they would have a harder time affecting the gravity-well, since the singularity was always positioned forward of the travel path, even with the ship flipped around. And with the speed of the *Arieel*, these two Klin ships were now out of the fight, unable to stay up with Adam's ship.

That still left two destroyers to evade. They'd seen Adam first maneuver and were moving into position to avoid a repeat. One would stay forward while the other took an angle off to the *Arieel*'s starboard side, ready to affect an EMP to the rear if necessary.

"Half a light to the Gate," Callie reported.

That didn't leave him much time to shake the pursuit, meaning Adam might have to become more proactive. As mentioned before, Adam did have weapons aboard, and one was a small rail gun that could fire metal projectiles at about a tenth light speed. That meant that if he intended to engage a target at light speed, he would have to be essentially wearing their skin. He would have to drop out of the well to make it work.

He primed the weapon and steered near the closest destroyer. The enemy ship matched vectors, accepting the challenge. They, too, had the same limitations while in light speed. They would have to dissolve their well in order to fire their flash weapons.

"What are you doing?" Callie asked from the co-pilot's seat. "Are you going to engage?"

"I'm going to concentrate, that's what I'm going to do. Please, timing is everything."

That didn't appease Callie, but mercifully, she remained silent, letting Adam focus on the job ahead.

Throughout his years of experience during countless space battles, Adam noticed a strange phenomenon that happened just before a well dissolved. There was the briefest of flashes as the singularity disappeared and the gravity-well rebounded to the relative flatness of normal space. It was the slimmest give away as to when a ship was committed to dropping out of a well. Adam was now staring intently at the space ahead of him, looking for that tell-tale sign. The Klin ship was invisible to him, being incredibly far away under normal circumstances, yet only seconds away at light speed.

Adam had seen the flash numerous times in the past before he realized what it meant. Even so, it wasn't always there. On the console next to the railgun control, Adam's fingers crossed. As he'd said to Callie earlier, he was all about skill. At the moment, he wouldn't mind a little luck.

And there it was—the flash!

Simultaneously, he dissolved his well and fired the railgun.

There's always a brief moment of disorientation when a body drops from light speed to normal space, be it organic or inorganic. The Klin aboard the destroyer were no exception. Adam could imagine what was happening on the bridge of the destroyer: As they quickly oriented to normal space, an alarm would sound. A mass object was directly in their path, and it wasn't the *Arieel*. It would be a ninety-pound chunk of steel traveling at a tenth light speed and carrying an incredible amount of kinetic energy. They wouldn't even feel it as the projectile tore completely through the ship along the stem to stern axis, ironically destroying the destroyer.

Adam only had a split-second window of opportunity to hit the Klin ship. Even a second's warning would have activated evasion controls and allowed the enemy vessel to avoid the projectile. Instead … splash another enemy vessel.

The last Klin destroyer was slightly behind the *Arieel*, having been guarding against another reversal maneuver. Now Adam could simply out-sprint it to the Gate.

Adam spun the *Arieel* around to the proper orientation and reenergized the gravity-well, shooting off again for the Devil's Gate.

"That was pretty cool," Callie said. She checked her screens. "We're about ten million miles out. You better start slowing down."

"That kinda defeats the purpose, doesn't it?"

"Dammit, Adam, there are dozens of ships out there waiting for passage. And then probably four or five trains within transit."

"I know. Let's just hope the gravity waves haven't changed much in the two days since we passed through the first time. The course is plotted into the auto pilot; all I have to do is avoid hitting anything."

"Our well is going to screw everything up."

"That's what I'm counting on. Now, please, time once again to concentrate."

Out the corner of his eye, Adam saw Callie flip him off.

Adam muted the CW comm so it wouldn't bother him. It was blowing up as controllers for both the Gate and for individual ships screamed at him, warning him off. Callie was right, there was a bottleneck of traffic waiting for passage or that had just arrived. It was like the end—or beginning—of the Suez Canal, and Adam's ship was about to race into it without permission, without a pilot and at full speed. What could possibly go wrong?

Vessels energized gravity-wells on an emergency basis and began moving out of the way. Others that remained stationary didn't stay that way for long. As the *Arieel* invisibly swept by at faster than the speed of light, they began to move, drawn inexorably toward the passing gravity source. Although none were drawn into the deadly maw, they did converge along a central line following the path of the *Arieel*. They weren't moving fast at the time, but a few of the vessels collided, while others activated chemical drives to avoid their neighbors.

And then Adam was within the Gate.

He reduced speed, bringing down well-intensity to a bare minimum to maintain an enveloping event horizon, the magic barrier that protected the ship and her occupants from the verities of Einsteinian physics. Even so, he was having a hell of a time keeping the *Arieel* on course, even on autopilot. Although invisible to the naked eye, space in the region was a confusing mess of eddies and whirlpools, ripples and towering crests, like the worst nightmare of a sea captain going around Cape Horn at the tip of South America. But worse than that, this crumpled up mess of space/time was in three dimensions.

It wasn't this bad coming in, which was a testament to the skill of the Gate pilots. They had equipment that constantly monitored the gravity in the region and instantly accommodated for it. Adam thought that since he had a map of the original route, it would be a piece of cake to follow. Now, he was having second thoughts. All kinds of second thoughts.

The *Arieel* spun over on its top. The idea of banking, pitch and yaw in a spaceship was counterintuitive in the days of weightless travel. But not with internal gravity-wells and inertial compensators. When a ship suddenly changed course, kinetic energy was still in play and the passengers felt the tug until their bodies reoriented. And with a pre-determined up and down, because of the internals, the ride through the Gate was ten times worse than the wildest rollercoaster on Earth—or anywhere else for that matter.

But Adam was committed. The only thing keeping the *Arieel* from being drawn into one of the competing blackholes was his own singularity and the forward momentum it provided. If his well dissolved, it would be all over. To either side of the Gate, gravity was too strong to escape, even with a well of their own.

And that's why each time the *Arieel* made an unexpected jerk to either side, the team thought they'd bought the farm. But with a combination of the autopilot dispassionately following the old channel, and Adam's constant tweaking of the controls, they managed to straighten out each time only seconds before it was too late.

And then there was the traffic they encountered along the way.

Fortunately, the Gate was wide enough for two gravity-drive ships to pass, but barely and only if they were expertly piloted. The *Arieel* wasn't being expertly piloted, only *luckily* piloted. This caused pileups of the two caravans Adam encountered. The train of five to ten ships each scrunched up and then became jammed in the channel, blocking the way, as gravity drives worked overtime to keep the vessels from drifting too far either way.

Adam was hoping for just such an outcome, although without as much drama. Blocking the Gate would keep the pursuit at bay. If the Klin did follow him into the Gate, his options would be greatly diminished with no maneuvering room. But now they were trapped on the other side. Adam had a clear shot at open—and safe—space. If he could keep the *Arieel* from being swallowed by a blackhole.

The passage is only about five hundred million miles., but it seemed like five hundred million light-years. Eventually, the strange twisting of space/time smoothed out and the *Arieel* spit out the other side of the Gate. But their adventure wasn't over.

There were hundreds of ships at this end of the Gate as well that were in harm's way of the rampaging spaceship. Fortunately, Continuous Wormhole communications are instantaneous and this Gate Control station had been warned from the other side. Most of the ships in a direct line with the entrance had been moved. For the others, Adam made some wild, split-second adjustments before the *Arieel* was beyond the staging area and into clear space.

Adam cranked up the well-intensity and sped away before anyone could stop them. He had no idea what laws he'd broken with his running of the Gate. If they were Klin laws, he was sure the silver-skinned bastards couldn't enforce them on this side. But he wasn't sure what the good guys here could do. There had to be rules against doing what Adam had just done, right? Either that, or no one was foolish enough to try, so why make it official with a regulation that read: "Thou shalt not risk one's life in a crazy, headlong run of the Devil's Gate. That would be stupid."

Adam smirked as he and Callie began the decompression after the run. At least Adam held the honor of being the person who proved it was possible to Run the Gate—and live to tell about it.

22

Nine hours later, the *Arieel* landed at the same spaceport on Lo'roan they'd left only three days before. A lot had happened since then, with very little of it satisfying. Before leaving the planet, Adam reserved a landing pad next to the *Farragut*, anticipating having to transfer millions of energy credits from one ship to the other. Now, the transfer was anticlimactic, and depressing.

The crew was not only mentally exhausted but physically beat up. The Gate Run had done a number on the Humans. Callie and Adam had bruises from their safety restraints, while Mike, Todd and Jay had been thrown around the common room after their barely functioning straps on the couch had broken. Jay even sustained a broken arm and was juiced up with pain meds, keeping him from helping with the loading.

The team had to get off Lo'roan as soon as possible. Although they'd shutdown the Clan counterfeiting ring, they'd also exposed corruption running to the highest levels within the security force and more-than-likely the government, as well. The original bounty had been initiated by rival factions, with both sides having their grubby alien hands in the pockets of criminal activity. No one was going to go down for this alone.

And then there was the question of Adam overstepping his authority. He was sure native attorneys were already working on the defense of the surviving counterfeiters, with Adam reading prominently in their briefs.

But now it was time to separate the bounty so the team could go their separate ways.

Eventually, they'd counted a crate and found that they did contain approximately five million in energy credits. After giving a crate away to the Arancus, each of the Humans was walking away with twenty million credits. Not a bad payday for three days of work. Not surprisingly, no one was celebrating.

Callie walked up to Adam on the field outside the *Arieel*, her red hair glowing in the afternoon light of Lo'roan. She hugged him tightly and then kissed him on the cheek. All the Humans were there, including Mike Hannon.

"Better luck next time, right?" she said humorlessly.

Adam smirked. "If so, then it should be third time's

charm. Our first two adventures together haven't been that profitable."

"Speak for yourself," Callie said with a wink.

Adam knew what she meant.

Mike came up, shook Adam's hand and then wrapped his arm around Callie's waist. She returned the gesture. Between the two lovers, they had forty million ECs. Now, that was a nice chunk of change.

Next came General Oakes. He gave Adam a powerful man hug and then shook his hand. "Thanks for running the operation, Captain Cain. In spite of everything, we didn't do too bad. If the damn Clan of the Hood hadn't shown up, things probably would have turned out differently. Adapt, improvise, overcome, that's a mantra for a reason. Seldom do missions go according to plan. It's the people who can go with the flow who come out winners."

"Funny, general, but I don't feel too much like a winner. And now I have to face Tidus. I'm not sure what he's going to do. I really screwed the pooch on this one. I lied outright. It will be a miracle if I keep my job."

"Hang in there buddy. If you need me to put in a good word for you with the Juirean, let me know."

"I don't think the testimony of a Human will carry much weight with him, but thanks for the offer."

Jay was sitting on a security crate at the back of the *Farragut*, his arm in a cast and still high on pain meds.

Adam's shoulder was almost completely healed already, but he wasn't going to rub it in. Besides, Adam envied the young man for all the drugs he had in his system. It would have been nice if Adam could just pop a few pills and his troubles would vanish. But he wasn't that kind of guy; never had been. He would buck up and face the music. He always had.

"I hope you can smooth things over with Tidus," Callie said. "Let me know. And along that note, Mike and I will be coming out to Tel'oran in a couple of months. The *Angel* is there and I need to pick her up, take her back to—" she looked up at Mike "—what's the name of the planet you live on … Avarice?"

"Navarus," Mike corrected.

"He says it's nice. He has a big house out at the end of a peninsula at the end of a crescent-shaped bay."

Mike grinned sheepishly at Adam. "Yeah; I picked it up for a song. It seems the prior owner just abandoned the home."

Adam wrinkled his face and nodded. He knew the place: it was his old home on Navarus. But he didn't say anything, leaving that up to Mike to tell her. Then he snorted. If the relationship lasted that long. He had a feeling Callie Morrison didn't stay in one place for very long. The galaxy was too big a place to put down roots.

Eventually, everyone boarded their ships and took

off. Oakes would drop Mike and Callie off at Navarus before he and Jay returned to Earth. And Adam had an appointment with Tidus. He owed him a call on the way back, which would give the Juirean plenty of time to design Adam's punishment.

As Adam set a course for Tel'oran he gave a sad shrug. At least he had a twenty million credit safety net. That would certainly lessen the fall.

23

Adam was nervous as a cat. He'd had three weeks to agonize over the upcoming meeting, playing dozens of scenarios through his head. And although the bank job had not turned out as planned, at least Tidus and Bandors Bank could be paid off using the proceeds from the counterfeiting job, getting both of them off his back. That's why Adam didn't hesitate this time meeting with Tidus only a few minutes after landing on Tel'oran.

As usual, the Juirean's countenance was hard to read. But Adam didn't care. He had more money than he'd had in a long time—at least since the currency changed from Juirean credits to energy credits. Sure, it wasn't anywhere near what he thought he get out of the Klin bank job, but it was better than nothing.

Adam kept telling himself that. It didn't seem to help calm his nerves.

"You seem pleased with yourself," Tidus said directly. "I don't know why. What was the final tally on the Klin raid?"

Adam was hesitant to tell him, but figured he'd find out sooner or later. He always did; in fact, he may already know and was testing Adam, as Tidus was wont to do.

"We each came out with twenty million."

"Not what you were counting on."

"It was supposed to be a lot more."

"It's always supposed to be a lot more. And in the meantime, you let a militant group of Kracori make off with the rest. Who knows what trouble that's going to cause for the galaxy."

"I'm not thrilled with it, either, but at least the job on Lo'roan went okay. I made enough money to pay you and the bank your million credits."

"Think again."

"What do you mean? I busted the counterfeiting ring and earned the million-credit fee. That's enough for your nine hundred thousand and Bandors' hundred."

"It would be … if the damn government of Lo'roan would pay it. As it turns out, they're not."

Adam was taken aback. "What do you mean they're not? I earned it!" Adam exclaimed.

Tidus puffed out a breath. "Apparently, you and your renegade Human friends got into a firefight in the middle of a high-class neighborhood full of expensive housing. Now, some of the residents are suing the government of Lo'roan for collateral damage, seeing that a few of their employees were in with the counterfeiters and you were a quasi-agent of said government. They're holding the government responsible."

"Good; they should be held accountable. Those backstabbing bastards almost got us killed."

"Well, the government is turning around and blaming you, and right now the matter is tied up in litigation. They're refusing to pay the fee until the matter is settled."

"Bullshit! They can't do that!" Adam was as mad as a hornet, but Tidus's passive demeanor helped calm him down. "We've run into this before, Tidus," Adam pointed out. "Collateral damage is covered in the contract. We get this all the time."

"With you I do."

Adam blinked. That was true.

"You're going to take these bastards to court, aren't you?" he asked.

"These bastards you speak of *are* the court on Lo'roan. And even if they win against the homeowners, they'll find some way to blame us—*you*—for starting the whole thing in the first place. And then they'll come after us—*me*—for punitive damages."

"So, what, you're just giving up?"

"That's right. This one I'm writing off. It's not worth the effort."

Adam leaned back in the chair. "Okay, then. I guess that's best. But at least I did my part. So, we're square, right?"

"Not even close."

"What do you mean?" Adam asked for the third time.

"You still owe me and the bank."

Adam nodded. He saw this coming, but at least this time he wasn't too worried about it. That would still leave him with nineteen million.

"That's cool; I'm anxious to get back on good terms with you. A million credits is a small price to pay for that." He grinned at the Juirean and began to get up out of the chair.

"Oh, I'm not through with you yet," Tidus said ominously. "Sit down."

Tidus ran his long fingers through the hair on the side of his elongated, green-skinned face before locking intense yellow eyes on the Human. "I warned you, Adam, about going rogue on me again. Over the past several months you've become increasingly unstable and unpredictable, a *burden* to the company rather than an asset."

Adam was in shock. He sat tense in the chair, his

mouth agape, wondering if Tidus was getting ready to fire him. It sure did sound like it.

"That is why I'm going to give you a choice. It's an either/or choice, no negotiating."

"What choice?"

"First, you keep your twenty million—now nineteen million after you pay me and the bank—and you leave the employ of Starfire Security. You also relinquish possession of the *Arieel*, which, as you know, is company property."

Adam's heart raced and his breath came short. He knew Tidus was pissed, but enough to fire him, to fire the only Human for hire he had on the staff? But the biggest shock was the *Arieel*. It was his home and had been for three years.

"And what's the other option?" he asked tentatively.

"That you pay back me and the bank and you keep your job … but you also buy the *Arieel* from the company for nineteen million credits."

"That's ridiculous!" Adam shouted. "That would leave me with nothing!"

"You'd have the thirty-eight thousand you have in savings. Oh, yeah, you spent thirty-three thousand of that on your most recent unsanctioned adventure. Dammit, Adam, every time you run off and do something you consider *off the books*, it still reflects on me and my company. You're *the Human*, and no matter what you do, you're linked with Starfire. I'm not sure I can afford the bad publicity any longer."

"I don't need to accept this," Adam huffed defiantly. "I could go to another security company. They'd be glad to have me."

Tidus snorted. "Will they, after what you've been doing recently? You're what you Humans call a *loose cannon*. Sooner or later you're going to cause a real shitstorm that you can't recover from. And any company you work for may not survive, either. Besides, if you go to another company, you'll need a starship if you are to do the job that would be expected of you. And you can't have mine—unless you pay for it. And I'm sure there aren't too many companies out there willing to give you a ship as advanced as the *Arieel*, and then let you keep it to live in it fulltime. I've done a lot for you, Adam, and this is the thanks I get; insubordination, chicanery and outright lies. I don't even know why I would consider keeping you onboard. But I am … at least under certain conditions."

Tidus paused and leaned back in his chair, steepling his fingers. "I know this is a big decision, so I'll give you a little time to make up your mind." He looked at the new clock resting on his desk. His old clock had been shattered into a million pieces a few months back when he threw it at Adam in a fit of rage.

Adam was frozen in place, his mouth still open and with a dozen things rumbling around in his mind. Yes, he had some money, but not a lot, not really. And if he left Starfire, he would have to give up the *Arieel*. Tidus was right, he would need another ship. And there would go the bulk of his money. And then there was the fact that Tidus more or less let Adam do his own thing—at least he used to—until Adam took advantage of him. And then there was—

"Time's up. What have you decided?"

Adam blinked and recoiled. "That wasn't much time."

"It wasn't really a choice, either. What will it be, Adam?" The Juirean grinned. "My way or the highway? I love Human slang; it is so … so creative."

"Don't you think nineteen million is a little high for the *Arieel*? Hell, I could buy a new one for twenty-five million."

"You could, but you don't have twenty-five million. Make up your mind, Adam. I'm busy and I don't have time to waste it on non-assets. Go or stay?"

"Fine, I'll stay, but you have to know I don't like this, not one little bit."

"Good. You're not supposed to like it. This is called punishment. Get used to it."

"You're leaving me with nothing, and after all I went through to get that twenty million. You have no idea."

"I also don't care. *You* made the decision to go after the Klin credits, not me. Now, live with it. And I suppose you're in need of some quick credits, so, I have an assignment for you."

"You do? Already? What if I decided to leave?"

"You couldn't leave. Now, let's move on. I have a juicy bounty hunt for you, something that might fit your current mood: A gangster with an army surrounding him. It should give you ample opportunity to smash some alien skulls and to vent some of that frustration you're feeling. I've already transmitted the details of the job to your computer. Now, hop to it, Mr. Cain. Go do your *Human* thing and make me some credits ... for a change."

When Adam got back to the *Arieel*, he was drained both physically and emotionally. He spent ten minutes walking from one end of the starship to the other and back again several times, to see if he felt any different now that the vessel was his. He didn't. He'd always considered the *Arieel* to be his, so this was nothing new. Maybe in a few days reality would sink in. But at the moment the only thing that was sinking in was the fact that he was flat broke. Tidus was right, he now had a little less than five thousand credits in his account. That wouldn't even buy a fully charged fuel pod. How did Tidus expect him to go after the bounty without a fuel pod? *Credit, that's how,* Adam cringed. He would have to go into debt with the Juirean again just to do his next job.

Is this what an indentured servant feels like?

Adam moved into the cockpit and sat at the pilot's station, accessing the file on his new assignment. The sooner he apprehended the fugitive, the better. At least then he'd have a little cashflow.

Just then, the buzzer sounded indicating an incoming link. Was it Tidus calling to light a fire under his ass? Adam wouldn't put it past him.

But it wasn't Tidus; it was Callie Morrison.

Adam was taken aback by the radiant face and halo of brilliant red hair. It had only been three weeks since he last saw her, and she never looked better. She was standing near a window, looking out at a crystalline ocean shimmering in the light of a new day, holding the communicator. Adam recognized the window; it was in his former home on Navarus.

"You look great, Callie," Adam said honestly. "So I take it things with you and Mike are going okay?"

Her eyes widened as if she was surprised. "Yeah, who would have thunk it? He's outside right now mowing the lawn."

Adam laughed. He looked out the viewport of the *Arieel* at the dull grey tarmac outside the ship. "At least you have grass to mow. Still, I never imagined Mike to be a home body."

"Me either, but he couldn't wait to do it. He said it's been twenty years since he last cut grass."

Callie read the unasked question on Adam's face. "He's really a sweetheart," she said.

"Are we talking about the same Michael Hannon; alien assassin and all-around scoundrel?"

"My kind of guy, I guess. But he's actually a pushover, a softy. Which means I'll probably grow bored of him in a few months and toss him away like so many others before him." Her smile was brilliant.

"That might be true … if there were more options available. As it is, you're probably the only two Humans on Navarus."

"Actually, there are six of us, but two are in prison so that doesn't count. Hey, the reason I'm calling is because Mike and I will be coming out to Tel'oran in about a month and we wanted to make sure you'd be in town. I have to pick up the *Angel* and do some shopping with our newfound wealth. Speaking of that, how was your reunion with the Juirean? Did you get him off your back? I still don't know why you would work for one of those green-skinned bastards anyway, but you must have your reasons."

"We go back a long way."

Adam saw Callie grin, reading her thoughts. A long time, indeed. Although Adam only looked in his early twenties; in actuality he was nearing sixty.

"And about the meeting," Adam continued. "It

went about as well as all the others I've had with Tidus." He went on to relate the events of the past two hours.

"That's horrible, and completely unfair!" Callie exclaimed; concern etched on her face. "After all your work, and you end up with nothing."

"Hey, I got the *Ariel*. That's something, I guess."

"But you already had her."

Adam shrugged. "You reap what you sow, as they say. I *have* been taking advantage of Tidus recently. It was bound to come back and bite me in the ass."

"But still; that sucks. What are you going to do now?"

"Get back to work. I already have a nice bounty-hunting job lined up—"

Adam saw Callie's expression go blank as a frown creased her forehead. She stayed that way for several seconds.

"Are you okay?" Adam asked.

She blinked and came out of the trance; the accompanying grin was strained.

"When's your birthday?" Callie asked unexpectedly.

"My birthday?"

"Yeah, the day you came into existence."

Adam laughed. "For me, that's not a simple question to answer. Do you mean the Old Adam Cain or the New? And then we'd have to know what day and month it is on Earth. Why do you ask?"

Callie's eyes were clouded. "Because I left you a present aboard the *Arieel*. Call it a birthday present—or Christmas—whatever."

"What is it?"

"It's a surprise, but I think you'll like it. Just don't get too mad at me when you see it. It's in the cargo hold, behind panel 128-C."

"Mad? Why would I do that?"

"You'll see. Anyway, Adam, I have to go now. Mike just finished up with the yard, and I wouldn't want him to think we're carrying on some illicit affair behind his back. It's only been a few weeks. That would be too soon, even for me. But maybe someday we can work another caper together. The last one was fun, in a macabre kind of way."

"Well, that's up to the Big Author in the Sky," Adam said. "But that would be nice. It was good seeing you again, Callie. You take care."

"I'll take it any way I can get it." And then she broke the link.

Adam was glad she called. It took his mind off the day's sudden and tragic turn of events.

But what was this present she left for him?

Adam went to the cargo hold and found the bulkhead panel she'd mentioned. Why hide a birthday present in the wall of the starship? Hell, why give him a present at all? He got the feeling there was more to the story than met the eye. What it was, he wasn't sure.

Reaching down into the dark crevasse, Adam pulled out an overstuffed backpack. He unzipped the top to find the bag was full of ... credits, energy credits. And a lot of them.

"What the hell?" he said aloud. His first thought was: *Are these counterfeit? Are these from Durin?* Instinctively, he knew that wasn't the case. These were genuine.

Adam's heart suddenly jumped into his throat.

No friggin' way! Could it be? God, I hoped not.

He raced to the common room where he spent the next twenty minutes sorting the chips and counting them. When he was done, he counted them another two times.

One million, six hundred thousand, forty-eight credits, the exact amount Mada's ten million was short.

Adam fell back on the couch, staring at the stacks of energy credits. He had it all wrong. They *all* had it wrong. Everyone except Callie Morrison. It was *she* who took the credits, not Mada Niac. She was the reason Tidus didn't get his recovery fee and why Adam ended up owing Bandors Bank. It was also the impetus why he joined the others to go after the Klin bank.

"That backstabbing, lying little—" he snarled.

But then Adam asked himself why she would give the credits to him now; in fact, why give them to him at all?

Guilt?

Probably not. She wasn't the type.

It had to be because she felt sorry for him after Adam told her about the meeting with Tidus. He shrugged. Good, at least someone felt sorry for him after his recent run of bad luck. It wasn't his fault, not all of it. And now this just proved it. It wasn't his fault the bank was shorted in their payoff.

Still, Callie had put him through hell.

But as much as he tried, Adam couldn't stay mad at her. It was hard to do while staring at one point six million in energy credits. It wasn't a lot, but it was enough to give him a little cushion and take the sting out of losing the twenty mil.

And he would be sure *not* to put the money in a bank where Tidus could track it. The Juirean would probably find some way to weasel it out of him if he knew he had it.

Instead, Adam Cain simply gave the stacks of money a little nod, and then with a wry grin, he said, "Well played, Callie. Well played."

The End

COMING NEXT...

Human for Hire (4)
Frontier Justice

Coming Next...

Get your copy today.

FACEBOOK GROUP

I'm inviting you to join my exclusive, secret, Super Fan Facebook Group appropriately called

Fans of T.R. Harris and
The Human Chronicles Saga

Just click on the link below, and you—yes, **YOU**—may become a character in one of my books. You may not last long, and you may end up being the villain, but at least you can point to your name in one of my books – and live forever! Maybe. If I decide to use your name. It's at my discretion.

trharrisfb.com

Contact the Author

Facebook
trharrisfb.com

Email
bytrharris@hotmail.com

NOVELS BY T.R. HARRIS

Technothrillers

The Methuselah Paradox
BuzzKill

Human for Hire Series
Human For Hire
Human for Hire 2 – Soldier of Fortune
Human for Hire (3) – Devil's Gate
Human for Hire (4) – Frontier Justice
Human for Hire (5) – Armies of the Sun
Human for Hire (6) – Sirius Cargo
Human for Hire (7) – Cellblock Orion
Human for Hire (8) – Starship Andromeda
Human for Hire (9) -- Operation Antares

Human for Hire (10) – Stellar Whirlwind
Human for Hire (11) -- I Am Entropy
Human for Hire (12) – Earth Blood
Human for Hire (13) – Capella Prime

The Human Chronicles Legacy Series
Raiders of the Shadow
War of Attrition
Secondary Protocol
Lifeforce
Battle Formation
Allied Command
The Human Chronicles Legacy Series Box Set

The Adam Cain Saga
The Dead Worlds
Empires
Battle Plan
Galactic Vortex
Dark Energy
Universal Law
The Formation Code
The Quantum Enigma
Children of the Aris
The Adam Cain Saga Box Set

The Human Chronicles Saga

Novels by T.R. Harris

The Fringe Worlds
Alien Assassin
The War of Pawns
The Tactics of Revenge
The Legend of Earth
Cain's Crusaders
The Apex Predator
A Galaxy to Conquer
The Masters of War
Prelude to War
The Unreachable Stars
When Earth Reigned Supreme
A Clash of Aliens
Battlelines
The Copernicus Deception
Scorched Earth
Alien Games
The Cain Legacy
The Andromeda Mission
Last Species Standing
Invasion Force
Force of Gravity
Mission Critical
The Lost Universe
The Immortal War
Destroyer of Worlds
Phantoms

Terminus Rising
The Last Aris

The Human Chronicles Box Set Series

Box Set #1 – Books 1-5 in the series
Box Set #2 – Books 6-10 in the series
Box Set #3 – Books 11-15 in the series
Box Set #4 – Books 16-20 in the series
Box Set #5—Books 21-25 in the series
Box Set #6—Books 26-29 in the series

REV Warriors Series

REV
REV: Renegades
REV: Rebirth
REV: Revolution
REV: Retribution
REV: Revelations
REV: Resolve
REV: Requiem
REV: Rebellion
REV: Resurrection

REV Warriors Box Set – The Complete Series – 10 Books

Jason King – Agent to the Stars Series

The Unity Stone Affair
The Mystery of the Galactic Lights
Jason King: Agent to the Stars Box Set

The Drone Wars Series
BuzzKill

In collaboration with Co-Author George Wier…
The Liberation Series
Captains Malicious